SPELLING DISASTER

USA TODAY BESTSELLING AUTHOR
HARPER A. BROOKS

Spelling Disaster © Copyright 2023 Harper A. Brooks

Visit my books at https://harperabrooks.com

All rights reserved. No part of this book may be reproduced, distributed, or transmitted in any form or by any means, electronic or mechanical, including photocopying, recording, or by any information storage and retrieval system, without permission in writing from the publisher/author.

This is a work of fiction. Names, places, characters and incidents are either the product of the author's imagination or are used fictitiously, and any resemblance to any actual persons, living or dead, organizations, events or locales is entirely coincidental.

Warning: the unauthorized reproduction or distribution of this copyrighted work is illegal. Criminal copyright infringement, including infringement without monetary gain, is investigated by the FBI and is punishable by up to 5 years in prison and a fine of $250,000.

H.A.B. Publications LLC

Cover Design: Danielle Fine with Design by Definition Covers
www.daniellefine.com
Interior & Formatting: Formatting by Jennifer Laslie
Editor: Read Head Editing

SPELLING DISASTER

Growing up as the daughter of a magical librarian, I've lived a thousand lives through books. When I'm supposed to follow family tradition and become a Cleric on my twenty-first birthday, the ancient library where I live mysteriously burns down and I'm named the main suspect.

To keep me out of trouble, I'm sent away to the Andora Academy of Witchcraft.

Cliques thrive at my new school, so of course, I'm at the bottom of the social ladder. But I have a much bigger problem than school drama. Something sinister is lurking in the shadows, something that wants to use me and my family for its devious plot.

I'm not the only one who's noticed, though. Theo, the popular witch I'm crushing on, knows too, and to my luck, he wants to help. Unfortunately, sifting through the academy's secrets is proving to be just as hard as passing my classes.

Scratch that—harder, and much more dangerous.

The closer Theo and I get to answers, the more dark

magic emerges. I may not have been able to save my home from the flames, but I refuse to let the academy, my family, and the truth all go up in smoke.

***Spelling Disaster* is an NA Paranormal Academy standalone.**

To my sanity,

Which left me a long time ago.

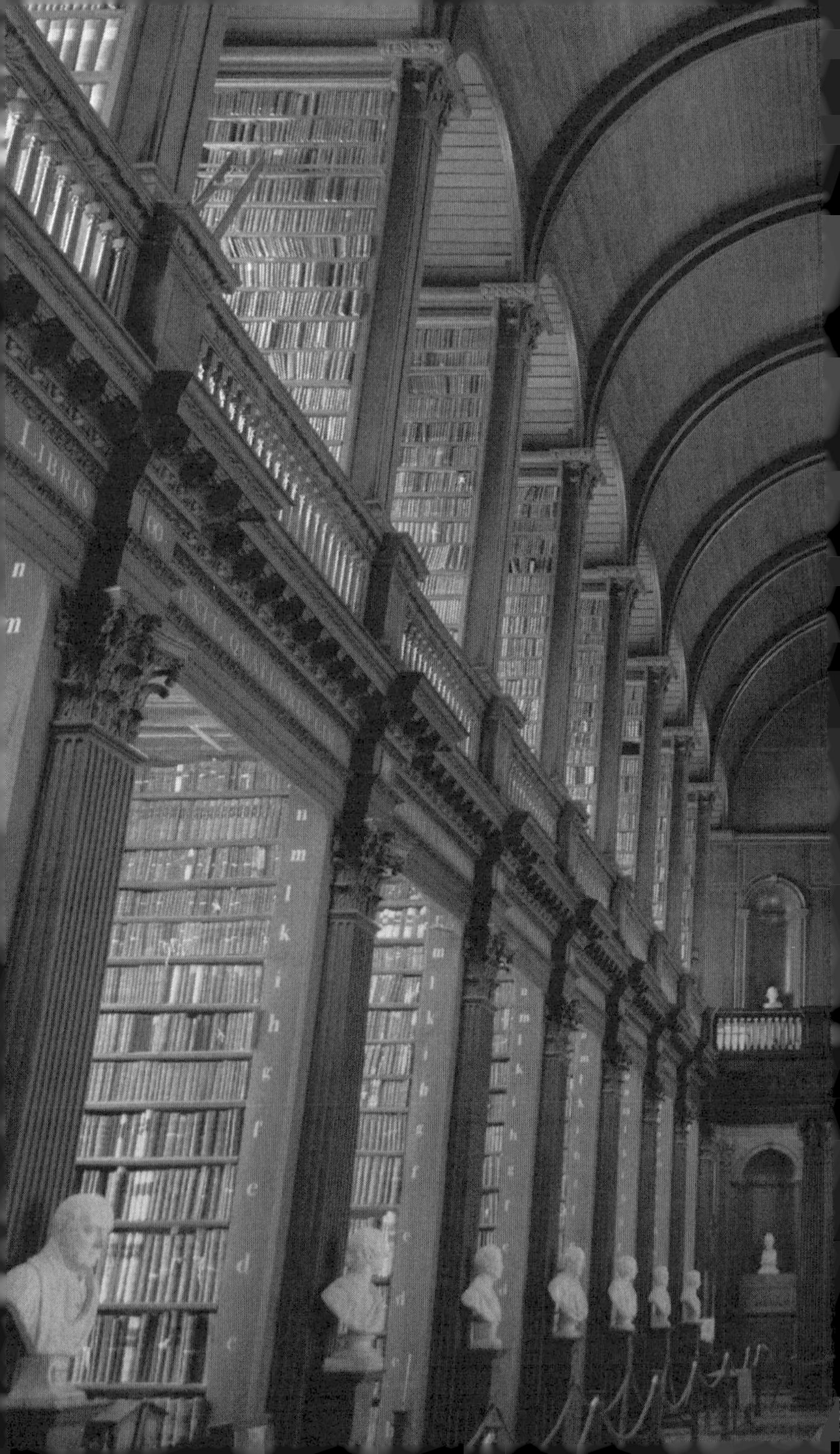

CHAPTER ONE

I jump from the romance novel, magic propelling me out of the pages and into the real world the same way it has a thousand times before. Sighing, I fall back on my bed with my heart thumping in pleasure, still clutching the open paperback to my chest.

"My. God," I say out loud.

Whisker twitch. Seconds later, a small furry body hops onto the pillow beside my head and the mouse scurries until he's sitting dead center on my chest. Staring at me in anticipation.

Bespelling myself into books takes a small spell and a little effort but there's so much to gain. It's worth every bit of energy and magic.

There's sweat on my brow and a smile on my face.

My familiar nudges me with his nose to get me to talk.

"It was glorious," I tell Gus. "I know logically that life in the Scottish Highlands is not all glamour and romance, but dang. Remi was right about this one."

You look like you enjoyed yourself.

Gus always knows how to read my mind, and it's a tool we use to speak to each other.

I gesture tiredly toward the book, needing a second to get my breath back but wow, what a rush. "It's a great book. There's romance and intrigue, not to mention gorgeous scenery. And Seamus."

Oh, Seamus. He'll forever have my heart.

I've never been one for Scottish romances, but my sister Remi loves them, and she's taken to sneaking them into the library for me to read.

Who would have thought? Yasmine Williams has a secret crush on men in kilts. Just like a normal girl! Although a normal girl would work in a library that actually stocks these kinds of books on the shelves.

Gus sniffs and offers me the mouse equivalent of a grin. *I'm glad you enjoyed yourself. At least you weren't gone for hours this time.*

"True. I love having a chance to actually explore a great romance." Something, if I'm being honest, I'll probably never get to experience in reality; not that I don't have hope it might happen for me someday. Emphasis on the *might*. Again, it goes back to the part about being a normal girl, and how I'm…not one. "I really wish a reality like this would, *could*, exist for me on this side."

The spells I use to dive into novels, even for such a small time, are only a reprieve. And not a permanent solution to my life path.

Not my life, I mentally correct. To my future.

I've been trained all my life for a future I'm not sure I want, but what other choices are there? Running a hand through my long, thick dark hair, I push up to a seated position and wait for the small swell of dizziness to pass.

Gus nudges me with his nose again. *You've got to get going. You're going to give your mother a heart attack if you're not downstairs soon.*

I glance at the clock, my heart thudding against my ribs and my eyes bulging out.

"Crap!" I scramble to right myself and fling Gus off the mattress in the process. My poor familiar. "I'm almost late!"

My mother is the most unforgiving boss I've ever had. She's the only boss I've ever had, unfortunately, and as the head librarian for the local witch coven, she tolerates nothing less than perfection from everyone beneath her. Especially me.

I wipe my eyes with the back of my hand to clear them, hard enough for stars to jump to life behind closed lids. A glance in the mirror assures me I'm doing all right. Not the best but I work with what I've been given. I spare a few precious seconds to rework my hair into a neat braid, pushing the baby fine black hairs away from my face. All eyes, I think, staring at myself. Eyes and dark eyebrows and golden tan skin to go with my exaggerated features.

I'm looking as well as can be expected after my romp in the heather with Seamus.

Oh, Seamus.

My toes curl inside of my sneakers. Remi had been right about him, too.

A reluctant antihero I can't help but adore.

This is my birthday present to myself. I offer my reflection a smile that warms the longer I think of the book. A few hours of uninterrupted fantasy to mark my special day.

"Okay, I've got to go. Thanks for watching my back!" I cast an apologetic glance over my shoulder to Gus before I bolt down the hallway.

My mom expects me down in the main library chamber on time. Even though it's totally my birthday.

Twenty-one. The big two-one where I've heard those normal kids go out and drink themselves stupid.

It's supposed to be an occasion marking the passage into adulthood. Or so I've read about mortal parties and coming-of-age stories.

Instead, I'll be working.

My footsteps are heavy as I make my way from our apartment in the rear of the library to the main chamber. Usually it's not so bad to work in the library with Mom. Today?

The tightness in my chest grows with each step and I shove the feelings of apprehension down deep. It's not bad on any other day but when it's my twenty-first birthday, with all the attached strings?

The book had been a gift to myself and a way to distract my mind from what I knew would come this afternoon.

Now that I'm back in reality, there are no more distractions.

SPELLING DISASTER

Mom has been acting strangely for the past few weeks leading up to today. Well, stranger than normal. Which means there *are multiple* strings attached because I'm the one she won't quite look in the eye. I'm the one whose questions always remain half answered or ignored entirely depending on the subject.

What can I expect? What's going to happen when I ascend?

Crickets.

My entire world is books and the characters brought to life on those pages. Mom made sure I'm well read, proficient in magic, and in complete control over my powers. None of those things help me figure out what happens to me today.

"Yasmine!" My name echoes through the hall and shoots straight to my rapidly beating heart. "You're late."

Mom calls out the last bit without having seen me yet and I hustle through the door with only a semi slump to my shoulders.

"I'm sorry," I begin. "I got caught up. I'm here now."

She's standing behind the giant oak main desk of the library with a pair of tortoiseshell glasses perched on the edge of her nose. It gives her the look of a studious model because her Middle Eastern heritage has helped her age more gracefully than any other coven member her age.

She doesn't need the glasses, either, and only uses them because she says it pays to look the part. It puts the others at ease. Who ever heard of a librarian who doesn't wear glasses or put their hair up in a bun?

"You *always* get caught up." Mom sweeps an arm out

at the looming stacks of books. "Stop messing around when there's work to be done. We only have another hour before it's time."

I want to ask: time for what?

What sort of celebration waits for me in an hour? The only thing I know is that I'm about to lose everything.

This is my real reality. I have to remind myself even when I'm struggling to find a common connection between me and the woman who birthed me.

Mom is…strict.

Overly strict.

She keeps us, me and my sister, completely isolated from the mortal world so that the only way we can get information is gossip or books. We're homeschooled and the only time we get out to socialize is when the coven meets.

Mom thinks her tales of horror regarding the human world will show us the dangers and help keep us safe. *The human world is full of things ready to cut you down and eat you alive.* So she says.

All I know comes from the romances and fiction Remi slips to me from her source. The romances and fiction I'm not supposed to read.

I hunch away from Mom and slink off to wash my hands before touching the books to restock. When I come out, Mom is helping a few coven patrons with their selections. She shoots me a look over the first woman's head and I automatically make my way over to her.

She's wearing a completely different expression by the time I get there. Like someone slipping off one mask and donning another, except the scowl she'd first greeted me with is the truth.

"I might be busy but never busy enough to wish this one a happy birthday," Mom tells the two ladies. "Can you believe it?" She beckons me over with a crook of her finger, kisses me on the cheek. Ruffles my hair in a way that makes me itch. "In one short hour you'll be twenty-one," she says.

My stomach sinks a little bit further. Turning that age at 2:45 p.m. on the dot today marks the end of everything I love, all the things I've enjoyed. It's the end of youthful magic and the ability that allows me to tap into said magic whenever I need to escape.

No more creating a playful fantasy escape.

As an adult, I'll have no choice. I'll have to put those things away forever even though I have no idea what waits for me once I do.

It's my duty.

It's an obligation.

And it's supposed to be an honor for some reason.

The women coo and remark about how wonderful it is for me to be this age. They talk about what I have to look forward to while my mother apparently glows with pride.

"Are you excited?" the woman on the left asks me.

I concentrate on the mole beside her mouth, more Monroe than Witch of the West. "Sure," I tell her, and the word turns to ash in my mouth.

"Of course she's excited," Mom answers for me. "She understands the gravity of this day as well. Sometimes Yasmine doesn't allow herself to fully express her emotions."

I blink at Mom. *I don't?*

The two women utter pretty much the same sound of comprehension before Mom pushes me off toward the rolling cart. "Go ahead and reshelve the stacks," she tells me.

I'm happy for any kind of exit and to take the one offered to me.

Except my mind won't rest. It spins around and around the fact that it's my birthday today and my birthday is nothing but the executioner's ax to the only joys in my life and no one to tell me why it's happening.

Still, I get to work pushing the cart through the stacks. The book on top is an occult history of eighteenth-century London.

It's one of the most popular items and we check it out with regularity.

I hum to myself as I find the right stack, but the sound dies soon after its birth. There in the stacks ahead—I know the hair, I know the slope of those shoulders.

I'd know Atlas even if I went blind because he gives off a certain air of power.

Currently, his hands are wrapped around the waist of my vastly more popular sister Remi. She's only a few years older than me but what a world of difference.

Enough difference that she has no issues finding a man and keeping him. A man like Atlas.

He's handsome, smart as a whip, and he makes Remi happy even though their hookups are a secret from Mom. She's not supposed to have a boyfriend, especially not a human one. Remi constantly sneaks him into the arcane section where she thinks they won't be bothered.

Which is true because sometimes their affections make me sick to my stomach. Today, I don't need any help there.

They both ignore me without giving me even a look.

The next hour zooms by as I reshelve and the clock counts down.

The air smells of dust and old worn book bindings as I mechanically bend and reach. Bend and reach. Sometimes I wish I was as free as Remi. Free to do what I want and be who I need to be and go wherever on a whim.

When it comes to magic, I got the payload, while Remi got the mortal half of our parents. Her lack of power leaves her free from the shackles of responsibility that I have, but I've never begrudged her the circumstances.

We can't help how we're born.

"Hey, yo." Remi reaches out from around one of the shelves and grabs my hand.

Startled, I drop the book I'm holding and it falls to the ground loud enough to make me wince.

"What's the matter?" I ask.

"I know you were watching. You can't tell Mom about Atlas. We were just talking," Remi insists. Her eyes narrow on me.

"Oh, yeah. I saw your mouths moving but no talking," I reply snarkily as I bend to grab the book.

Remi's scowl deepens and the expression is so 'Mom' I know I'll never be able to tell my sister without her freaking out. "When it comes to boys, they can be complicated," she continues. "And since you're at the age where you might actually meet someone, let me offer you some advice."

I shake my head. "I really don't need advice." Like I'll be getting into a relationship anytime soon? Definitely not.

"Even in your books, the heroine has some transformation to do. The same applies to men," Remi continues. "There are times you have to change something about yourself in order to fit in."

The advice rankles and feels wrong.

"I have no need to change for anyone." Something about the statement irks me, burrowing beneath my skin.

Change?

What did my sister think I needed to change, and why?

Her eyes scour me from top to bottom. "I love you, Yas, but hiding out in your marm-like attire isn't going to get you the happily-ever-after you desire or deserve." She's trying to soften the blow. Which I can appreciate.

Especially, I admit, when she is right.

I replace the book on the shelf and tug on the hem of my shirt. It's a black-and-yellow plaid button up. It doesn't gap at the breasts and it's really comfortable with all the moving I have to do. Complete with jeans and my well-worn All-Star sneakers...she might be right.

I'll never let her know.

"What's wrong with this shirt?" I ask her.

Remi sighs. "It's not the shirt. It's everything."

She takes off and leaves me in a puddle of hurt feelings. I'm not hiding here. I'm living out in the open the best way I can. Besides, I have responsibilities. Remi has no clue what it's like to be the one shouldering them. Like getting the work done. The stacks in the cart aren't shrinking and I'm the only one around to make sure it's done.

T-minus fifteen minutes before it's time for my birthday celebration.

I make it through one entire stack of books on the cart and halfway through the second when one of the books slips down from the shelf, one I hadn't touched.

A tattered grimoire.

Automatically bending at the waist, I reach for it. Stop. My stomach does a strange flip.

I've never seen the book before.

Straightening, I stare at the cover and the intricate lines of silver embossing around the title. There's no author name available but it's clearly old. Older than a lot of the stuff we have here.

A shiver runs through me.

This one...doesn't feel right. There's something wrong about it. Something I can't put my finger on. I hesitate to use the word *evil*—

This thing is supercharged with something bad, though, a tangible darkness I feel buzzing and warm beneath my fingertips. The sensation washes over me and I shiver, but not with the chill.

For some reason, it draws me in and makes me want to read.

CHAPTER
TWO

*N*o. A small voice in my head gets louder by the second. It has to in order to drown out the very odd sensations begging me to open the book and see what the contents hold.

Don't do it.

I'm suddenly not sure which of the voices belong to me—the one telling me to put the book down and back away slowly or the one begging me to read. Slowly, infinitesimally, one of the voices drowns out the other.

The book spine burns my fingers and yet I'm physically unable to put it down. The silver letters along the front glisten in the low light and the air around me quickens and moves like breath from a body. An invisible wind blows and I feel the force of it in my bones, hear it howling in my ears.

There's no looking away.

This is something special. What's it doing here?

I've never seen it before, and I'm willing to bet it's

not on any inventory list, either. I also know better than to touch things like this. Know better than to let myself be swayed by any kind of unnatural magic and this is nothing if not unnatural. Books don't show up out of nowhere and drop out of thin air. I know better.

Mom made sure I did.

I should drop the thing where I stand but—

I'm curious about it and how the thing found itself on the stacks. Too curious, even. Pushing past the *oogie* sensations rolling off the book in waves, giving into the need inside of me, I press it to my chest and sneak around to a corner of the library where I won't be disturbed to scrutinize it. To take a closer look. Especially when I stop and hold the book in front of me only to have it open up to a page at random, on its own.

The shock is nearly enough to have me drop it.

What the hell is this thing?

I glance left and right and once I'm sure I'm alone, I flip back to the page.

My heart freezes in my chest.

It's about the ceremony, the one taking place today. For me. For my birthday celebration. Here are the answers I've been wanting that Mom has been so wholly unwilling to give me beyond advice to be grateful.

To say silent thanks because magic like mine does not come along often.

I shift my finger along the page and read the words silently to myself. Odder still that they're in plain English and easily legible.

At the age of twenty-one, the witch will lose her childhood magic and ascend into the caste of Clerics.

This is the pinnacle of the learned for the coven.

Only those with the power can ascend to the caste of Clerics and only the chosen one may amplify said power with the help of the coven. The loss of childhood magic is a test of dedication and, should the witch be willing, be replaced by magic infinitely greater.

Changed.

The shadows press in closer around me and my heart thuds out a vicious beat. Having to lose my childhood magic isn't anything new to me. It's the one thing about today Mom has told me about, in preparation.

But what is this about the caste of Clerics?

Mom has only ever said good things about the Clerics before, about how I should be proud to be the one chosen to ascend. It's why she's been training me with such dedication. Hours and hours of spellcasting and bookwork. Hours more in which she claimed she had to put me through my paces for my own good.

Everything I've learned about witchcraft until this point has come from the path my mother set me on. For all I know, the Clerics are the keepers of the words and nothing more.

Yet this book, wherever it came from, hints at something else.

Something darker and inescapable. My fingers stick to the page and I'm unable to pull them away even when I want to stop. This, I think to myself. This book somehow has all the answers I've been looking for.

I skim the page.

The caste of Clerics is sacred, and such the duty of the one chosen to ascend. Power unmeasured. On the day of birth at twenty-one years, the witch—

I purse my lips in disappointment. The text gives me no further details to go on and yet I can't stop reading and no matter what I say to myself, I can't look away.

All along, a part of me suspected there was more going on with my birthday today, but nothing Mom has told me led me to believe the Clerics would be involved.

Or that joining them would be anything but a good thing.

What does it really mean to be a part of their group? Is today more than just an initiation? Is giving up my magic the equivalent of a hazing ritual to join their special club?

Most of all, I want to know what happens next.

I scour the book page repeatedly and turn to the next to see if there's anything else written on the subsequent page. There's nothing except the two paragraphs in the scrawling script.

I close the book slowly and stand there for a long moment breathing, struggling not to freak out.

In all my years, I've never seen an ascension ceremony. No one has given me any indication of what to expect, since somehow my birthday will be different from others in the coven. Not like we're a huge coven, either. Aside from my sister Remi, who's excluded from coven activities with her lack of magic, there are only two others who are close to my age.

"Come on," I mutter out loud, flipping back to the

right entry in the strange book. "There's got to be something you can tell me. Something more."

Right there.

I see a small notation on the bottom right corner of the page.

"If the ascended should wish to keep her light magic," I say out loud, "she should make an offering to the Horned God. Only he can see the task through."

The next page has an illustration of the Horned God himself. No, an *engraving*, of a masked man with large antlers. His features are human underneath the mask but whoever did the engraving made it seem as though the antlers curve right out of his skull. His chest is bare, covered in all sorts of symbols I don't recognize, and what can only be described as a loincloth covers his lower half.

The lines of his body, the curve of his muscles—the Horned God is all masculinity and feral grace. His shoulders hunch forward slightly as though any second will have him stepping directly out of the page.

I run my finger over the engraving and wince at a sharp flash of pain. The paper cut me! Wincing, I pull back, staring at my index finger and the small hole in the flesh.

A drop of blood wells up from the wound, dropping onto the page, being absorbed as quickly as it appeared.

"Shit." I stick my finger in my mouth and suck at the wound to keep any more blood from spilling.

Mom has strict rules about sullying the books, her control slipping over so that she expects everyone to keep them in pristine condition. And although I'm not sure where this one came from, if she sees me here, she'll flip.

Blood is an absolute no-no.

Soon the sting of the wound eases and when I pull my finger from my mouth, the bleeding has stopped.

The air rushes from my lungs and my head tips back on my neck, eyes rolling into my head as a vision sucks me under in my next heartbeat. No time to be afraid. No time to ground myself to understand what's happening. I'm still gripping the book as I go under and soon even that sensation fades under the rush of the vision.

It unfolds inside my head and I see a dark forest.

The details are crystal clear and the rudeness of the scene, the vividness, scares me. Naked tree limbs reach toward a black sky broken only by the light of the twinkling stars and the outline of the new moon.

I'm not just seeing the forest, I'm inside of it. The pulse of the earth beneath my feet is something tangible, the energy traveling up my legs and nestling somewhere in my core. Night creatures hum and the sky overhead is broken by the flapping of bat wings.

Shapes flicker in and out of reality, slowly solidifying into human men and women dancing around a bonfire. Masks hide the wearers from recognition.

It's madness.

It's life and chaos and everything I haven't been allowed to experience. Fear turns to a ball of lead inside of me, along with another emotion I hardly feel comfortable naming. *Desire.*

How would it feel to dance with them? To experience such unbridled freedom that it doesn't matter whether you have clothes on or not? It doesn't matter what people think of you.

No one wears clothes and their bodies writhe in what I hope is a dance and not some kind of ritual. It's like no dance I've ever seen before though. It's savage and brutal and intoxicating. They have no mind for anyone else and no heed for what they're doing outside of their own pleasures.

In the vision, my feet step unerringly toward the bonfire. Its heat and life are a beacon in the darkness as though there's nothing for me to be afraid of out there.

This forest is mine even though I've never been there before.

The monsters are only people out in the open with their breasts and genitals on display. They fling their arms out to their sides and overhead, stomping their bare feet into the moist dirt around the flames.

Full of life, promise.

Magic.

And there, just outside the ring of light around the flickering blue and amber, is the outline of horns. They rise and cast darkness against the tree trunks behind the man, the god.

The one from the engravings.

He's even more massive standing in front of me. The muscles in his arms and chest are cut from stone and his fingers flex at his sides. Each inhale has his chest heaving like a beast who's run the gamut and sweat sheens along tanned gold skin, dripping down toward the loin cloth lined in fur.

I'm not sure what freaks me out more: the sight of him, the sight of blood on his palms, or the way I want to go to him.

I'm captivated.

It's primal anarchy and nothing I've been allowed to experience before. Nothing I've been allowed to even *consider* wanting or turning toward because I've never been given a choice.

These people all choose to follow the beat of their blood.

If given the same choice, would I want to be in their position? Dancing for this god and his delights?

The smoke is in my lungs and in my nose, my mind, turning the outside world into a distant dream and this scene into reality. There's no thinking, only feeling. No worries outside the beat of my heart and the Horned God.

Despite the mask he wears, I know he's looking directly at me.

Blood brought me here and the Horned God is demanding a sacrifice from me. What am I willing to give up in order to keep my magic? He can make it happen. If anyone can offer me this lifeline, it's him.

I have no idea what I'll gain if I make one, or what I'll lose.

"Yasmine? What are you doing? Yas, answer me!"

My mother's voice pulls me out of the vision like a hook through my middle and I come back to my body with a gasp. Hastily, still blinking to shed myself of the fog of the bonfire, I shut the book, shoving it underneath one of the back shelves as I struggle to catch my breath.

Holy shit, what just happened to me?

The vision felt tangible enough that it's taking me much longer to feel at home in my reality. The only reality, I reason. The vision wasn't real, despite how my lungs feel burned and filled with the taste of wildness.

"Yasmine, I swear..." Mom trails off. "Where are you?"

I hurry toward her, following the sound of her disappointment and find her waiting for me with her foot tapping against the floor back where I'd been when I first discovered the book.

"I'm here," I tell her. The hasty smile I plaster on my face is hardly convincing.

She scours me from top to bottom with a look, and an arch of her right brow tells me exactly what she thinks of my appearance.

"You're lollygagging again?" she asks. "Today of all days?"

I shake my head. "I'm finishing up the cart, Mom. I just didn't hear you calling me. Sorry."

A loud ticking fills my ears, as though a heart is beating underneath the floorboards of the ancient library. Why hadn't I noticed it before?

My own heart times with it until they beat in tandem and it's a wonder Mom can't hear either one.

"Why do you look as though you've run a marathon, then?" Mom presses. She taps her foot waiting for an answer but her taps are at odds with the ticking, threatening to drive me mad.

Do I tell her? Or not?

She knows more about the magic world than I do as she's been a part of it for longer. Going out on a limb, I decide to share. "Actually, it was the strangest thing. I had a vision—"

The ticking grows louder as Mom shakes her head and interrupts with, "Honey, we really don't have time for your fantasies." She points over her shoulder. "I need your help. I've got a line at the front desk and there are way too many people for me to handle by myself. Everyone is here for your birthday celebration."

"Mom, I'm trying to tell you. I grabbed a book and I saw this scene in my head, with people around a bonfire—" I start to say again, too distracted to think straight.

"You'll tell me later, Yas. Okay?" She turns and heads off in the opposite direction. "Once we finish with these patrons, then I need you to go grab Remi and get ready. We're on a schedule."

She's paying no attention to me.

Whether the vision was real or not, a glance at the clock at the front of the library shows me I'm officially twenty-one in five minutes.

"Happy birthday to me," I whisper.

My head hangs heavy as I follow after Mom, the ticking getting louder and louder with each passing second.

No matter how many people I greet, or books I check out, I can't shake the image I've seen from the book. Was it really a vision like I first thought? Or worse. A prophecy of what is to come?

My ears are ringing.

I'm reading too many far-fetched stories. The ringing in my ears almost seems like a warning that something is about to happen. The air thickens and I tense, an ache starting in my tightening chest.

Nothing about this day is unfolding the way I thought it would. Maybe I should have found a way to try and extend the spell to keep me in the Scottish Highlands with Seamus. At least then I'd be having fun rather than feeling like I'm one step ahead of my doom.

The ticking continues, louder than before and now it's almost indistinguishable from the roar of my blood.

I help Mom make it through the line of avid readers, all of them stopping to wish me happy birthday before they leave for the ceremony. Or, as the last witch said, *picking up something special before it's time*.

Somehow I manage a tight smile for each one of them until it's only Mom and me alone in the library again.

She reaches beneath the desk to grab a placard and flips the light switch behind her on and off in rapid succession to let any stragglers know it's time to get out.

I turn to her and say, "Since we're alone, I want to talk to you about something." My tongue feels three sizes too large and desert dry in my mouth. "Please. It's important."

"I'm sorry, honey, but it's got to wait for another time. We're heading to your ceremony." She stops only to look around and narrow her eyes. "We've got to get

Remi. Do you know where she is? You were supposed to go and get her."

When? Before or after Mom wanted me to help her with the checkouts? I open my mouth to say exactly that when Remi shows up.

"I'm here, I'm here." My sister rolls her eyes. "Don't get your panties in a twist, okay, Mom?"

"You're going to get lippy with me today, of all days, young lady?" Mom asks, her tone chilled in warning.

It's the same song and dance as every other day with them. For some reason, I thought things might be different on my birthday, yet here we are with the tension thickening.

Remi flips her hair over her shoulder and cocks a hip, almost daring Mom to say something. About her, about me, about anything at all.

Mom finds something to complain about regardless of the circumstances. She finds fault with too many sunny days in a row. "All right, then. We're all here." Mom's hands go to her own hips and she glances between the two of us with an expression sharp as a scalpel. "Let's go."

In her next breath she loops her arm through mine, practically dragging me away. The book is on the shelf somewhere behind me and yet I still hear the heartbeat in the stacks. In the foundation and the walls of the building.

When I glance over my shoulder one last time, the air in the library grows visibly foggy, and I know it isn't my imagination. Smoke tendrils creep along the lines of the wood floor and around the tall stacks, climbing up toward the ceiling.

"Mom, there's something wrong." I shake my head and my ears grow warmer, like someone's stuffed them full of cotton. "Do you see the fog? Why don't you see it?"

"See what?" she asks.

Her voice clangs through me, at a distance even though she's right in front of me.

The fog is more dense than regular smoke and it's curling up the shelves with a mind of its own, thick and cloying. Reaching. Each step I take in the opposite direction has the strange ticking sounding louder, louder as the fog reaches for me.

Unbearable.

My stomach fills with heat.

A sense of wrongness invades every cell in my body and although I call out for Mom, for Remi, neither one of them hears me.

CHAPTER
THREE

The air in the main chamber of the library stills until every step I take, every step Mom and Remi take, is in slow motion. There is only the beat and the fog and the pull in my gut unwilling to let me go.

"Mom..." I trail off.

Black dots dance at the corner of my vision, and when I look in their direction, Mom and Remi are partly frozen in place. It's only me and the sick churning sensation in my gut that I can't shake.

"I had a vision. There was a book, and it dropped out of nowhere. Mom, I've never seen it before." I have to rush to get the words out, hoping, praying, she'll finally listen. "The book was strange and when I opened it, the vision came over me. Almost like I'd been meant to find that book. Mom!"

There's no indication she hears me. Mom's face is blank, and Remi's is frozen into a mask of apathy. She's standing several steps to the side. Too slow. The world is too slow and I'm the only one going at normal speed, with the very abnormal heartbeat of the room. The air itself pulses in time with the sound.

"Do you see this?" I ask her. "What's going on? Please tell me you see this. The vision wasn't normal, Mom."

Remi turns like she's wading through water, her expression shifting into one of confusion, and doesn't answer.

My words fall on deaf ears.

I wave a hand in front of her and she slaps it away so she can see me, her time and my time finally colliding. It rushes over me all at once, leaving me breathless. She just can't—

"What the hell is the matter with you?" she snaps, gaze harsh. "You're acting really weird, weirder than normal for you, Yas."

I reach for her again and this time she makes contact. Everything around me is normal again, but her slap does nothing to ease my fears.

"You think because you're finally old enough to drink that you can somehow have a mental breakdown?" she asks.

"Remi, I had a vision," I try to say.

"Sure, okay," she replies, snarkier than ever. "Whatever you say."

No one will listen. No one will pay me any mind and when I reach out to grab Mom's shirt, to get her to stop, she keeps going on autopilot.

"Come on, girls," she commands woodenly. "We need to go."

I've never had the type of magic that allows me to

see the future or sense what other people are thinking and feeling. It's not in my wheelhouse despite my gifts.

I've only had my intuition to rely on until now, not that I trust myself. There have always been too many voices in my head, and all of them sound like Mom, telling me she's the one who makes the decisions.

The one who has to prepare me for whatever I'll face.

She's the one I trust. My master.

I'm the apprentice who will never be as confident and powerful as she is. But right now, I'm the only one I've got and the world around me has warped.

Rather than stopping and taking stock of the situation, we're outside in seconds.

Remi falls into step beside me and both of us trail a foot behind Mom.

She leads the way out of the library and the afternoon light turns the entire world golden. Twilight will be on us soon and Mom's military steps lead across the parking lot toward the trees lining the property edge.

Inside those trees is our sacred circle, the one the coven uses to perform ceremonies. I've been there too many times to count but today everything feels changed.

Sweat breaks out along my spine and hairline. My heart throbs faster with each step we take away from the library and I'm about a second away from panicking. Or puking.

Remi calmly walks beside me with her shoulders thrown back and not a care in the world. Her cheeks have blossoms of color, pink against her dusky caramel skin, and her hair longer and wavier than my own.

"Remi, look at me." I'm begging her. "Look at me and tell me you don't feel like something isn't right."

She shakes her head and keeps walking into the dim hush of the woods.

This isn't the way things are supposed to go and my family should definitely be able to hear me. To understand me.

"We have to stop. We shouldn't go through with this," I say.

Except for some reason, I keep walking, my body betraying me. I need a moment to think, to figure this out. Reality still feels thin, as though there's something lurking at the edges of my consciousness, insistent for me to turn away.

The feeling makes focusing on the ceremony impossible.

The tree trunks press thick against each other, their limbs filled with leaves on the brink of turning for autumn, a soft breeze rustling them together. A few more steps and the trees open up into a clearing.

There is a sense of the familiarity in this place, of agelessness. Until this point, I always saw it as a quiet place to come when things got a little stressful at the library. Or when Mom is being particularly hardheaded about anything and everything.

Only me, the breeze, the forest. Time to clear space in my head.

The trees make a perfect circle to let the light of the

sun shine down on the grass and moss at the center. I've danced there.

I sang and chanted and joined the other witches for holidays and celebrations.

Today it's for me and there's nothing magical about it now.

Birds continue to sing and chirp as they do on any other day and there I stand in a cold sweat with clammy hands and ants crawling underneath my skin. Thoughts and memories of my vision tangle together with the coven waiting to welcome me with open arms.

I recognize most of their faces but there are a few others who I've never seen before, those who must have come from the coven in the next town. Just to celebrate my birthday and the ascension ceremony.

I gulp, my stomach empty and rolling.

What would I give to turn back the clock? To be seventeen again? Twelve?

I glance over to Remi and for an instant I feel nothing but jealousy for her—a wave of dark, ugly feeling. What would I give to have her mortal blood instead of the witch powers I'd inherited?

But I need her here with me. I need her strength and determination more than I'm willing to admit.

I reach for her hand.

Time speeds up at last and the thrumming of the invisible heart—definitely not my own—grows unbearably loud.

Applause and voices lifted in congratulation are not enough to rival the ticking beat.

Someone drapes a long cloak over my shoulders and

as the witches gather behind me, a set of hands push me toward the center of the clearing. I glance over my shoulder in time to see Remi shake her head, her eyes deep and a little scared, before she darts back toward the library.

Only the dark end of her ponytail is visible before she disappears entirely.

"Remi!" My voice is lost in the din.

She abandoned me.

She left me here with the rest of these people, all smiling and cheerful, who don't seem to see that there is something seriously freaky happening. The unnatural fog wraps around the trunks of the trees along the clearing and halts as though it's unwilling to go any further.

My chest tightens.

"Mom?" I turn in a circle and find myself unable to move with the press of so many people. "Mom, where are you?"

Lost in the crowd, lost to me, having led me to the chopping block only to drop me and leave.

"We're gathered here today for Yasmine! We celebrate she who takes the first step into adulthood and willingly chooses to embrace her path as the newest Cleric!" Our high priestess Lark lifts her voice to the heavens above, clear as a bell, which does nothing to stem my anxiety, as it has in the past. "Today Yasmine will relinquish her childhood to welcome her future."

I shake my head. *No.*

The other witches are dressed in their ceremonial robes with the hoods over their head, obscuring their features. Like the one I'm now wearing—moons and stars stitched in silver thread stand out against black velvet.

I'm drowning.

Why don't they see me drowning?

The others press closer in a ring around me, their bodies blocking my vision. There are too many hands. Too many cloaks to see past. The one over me is stifling and hot even with the crisp chill of this early October day.

I can't breathe.

"Mom, the vision," I try to call out, willing her to hear me no matter where she is now.

The ticking is loud enough that I feel like I'm screaming to be heard.

"In my vision I saw a bonfire, and a horned god. There were people dancing and I've never seen the book before!" I rush to get it out, hoping and praying someone will understand and stop this.

A sense of foreboding hits me hard enough to make me choke.

The sound of the beating heart is louder, closer.

Is it my fear? Is it nerves? Is it selfishness because I really don't want to give up my magic? Or is it the damn book, thrumming from within the library's walls and unconfined by logic or physics?

"Focus on the ceremony. You're supposed to be here, Yasmine. There is nothing to worry about." Mom's voice comes through, strange and dreamy. The tone is completely unlike her. "This is your destiny! Only you can ascend."

"Only you," the coven repeats in perfectly ordered unison.

"Things are going as planned." And she's still ignoring me and insisting things are fine. "Stop worrying. You will not ruin this ascension," Mom continues.

The tone sounds like her a bit more, though, always chastising me.

I jerk to the right, hearing her like she's next to my ear, only she's not there. She's nowhere and when I break away from the hands holding me, they reach, grab, tighten and hold.

I shake my head and dig my heels into the ground. The person behind me practically shoves me toward the man waiting in the center of the clearing. Our High Priest, Eli.

He nods reassuringly at me while the members of the coven take a step in the opposite direction. A sweet faced, round cheeked man in his mid-fifties, he came to our coven over a decade ago to take the place of our last high priest. He and Lark aren't a couple in any romantic sense, although they embody the archetypal divine masculine and feminine.

"Welcome, Yasmine," he says.

The coven circles and begins to chant low under their breath, words of welcome to lay the foundation for the ceremony.

"This isn't right. Something happened to me in the library. I don't want to do this," I tell Eli. My chest tightens to the point of pain and my stomach drops between my feet. I turn to whoever will listen at this point.

The witch to my right has her eyes closed, lost to her chant, the Latin syllables flowing freely. The fog remains trapped around the outside of the sacred circle, flickering like gray flame.

"Please," I sob. "Please. We have to stop. This isn't right!"

Between the ticking beat and their chant, timed perfectly with the rhythm, I'm going out of my mind. My head aches.

I grab my ears, knees shaking hard enough to send me teetering sideways. They don't hear my warning, no one does. Something is coming and they're too caught up in their chanting frenzy to listen.

They seriously have to stop.

My lungs seize, throat swelling until I'm struggling for air.

"This is how it's meant to be, Yas," Mom continues. "It's your birthday. You will ascend."

Like it being my birthday makes any kind of difference. No one will listen to me even though we're all going to be affected. I know it, just as I know the heartbeat is a countdown to whatever bad thing is about to crash down on our heads.

We're all waiting to be driven under and accept our fate blindly.

Eli holds his hands out on either side of my head as Lark steps around to my side with her hands on my shoulders.

"We welcome the chosen," the two of them chant.

His eyes roll back in his head. The spell bursts to life in a large glowing ball in front of my face until it stretches into the familiar shape of a five-pointed star. Each point is supposed to stand for the elements of earth, air, fire, water, and spirit. A circle of protection to amplify the magic of the user.

The exact spell that's going to take away my magic before I'm ready to give it up. Birthday or no birthday.

He sketches a circle around the pentagram in the air until the entire design sparks. Several other coven members hold candles in front of them with the wicks lit and flickering.

"Stop! Please, stop it!"

I'm crying.

It's no use.

"Hold her steady," Eli calls out.

Two of the coven members step on either side of me and Lark shifts to my rear, all three of them taking my arms to keep me still. They force me down to my knees while the magic pulses overhead.

Magic grows around us, starting to work, and the space inside me where it's always dwelled feels empty.

Something shifts behind the High Priest and through the magic haze, through the rolling fog, I see it. *Him.* The Horned God in his mask and loincloth stands inside the shade of the trees, smiling at me.

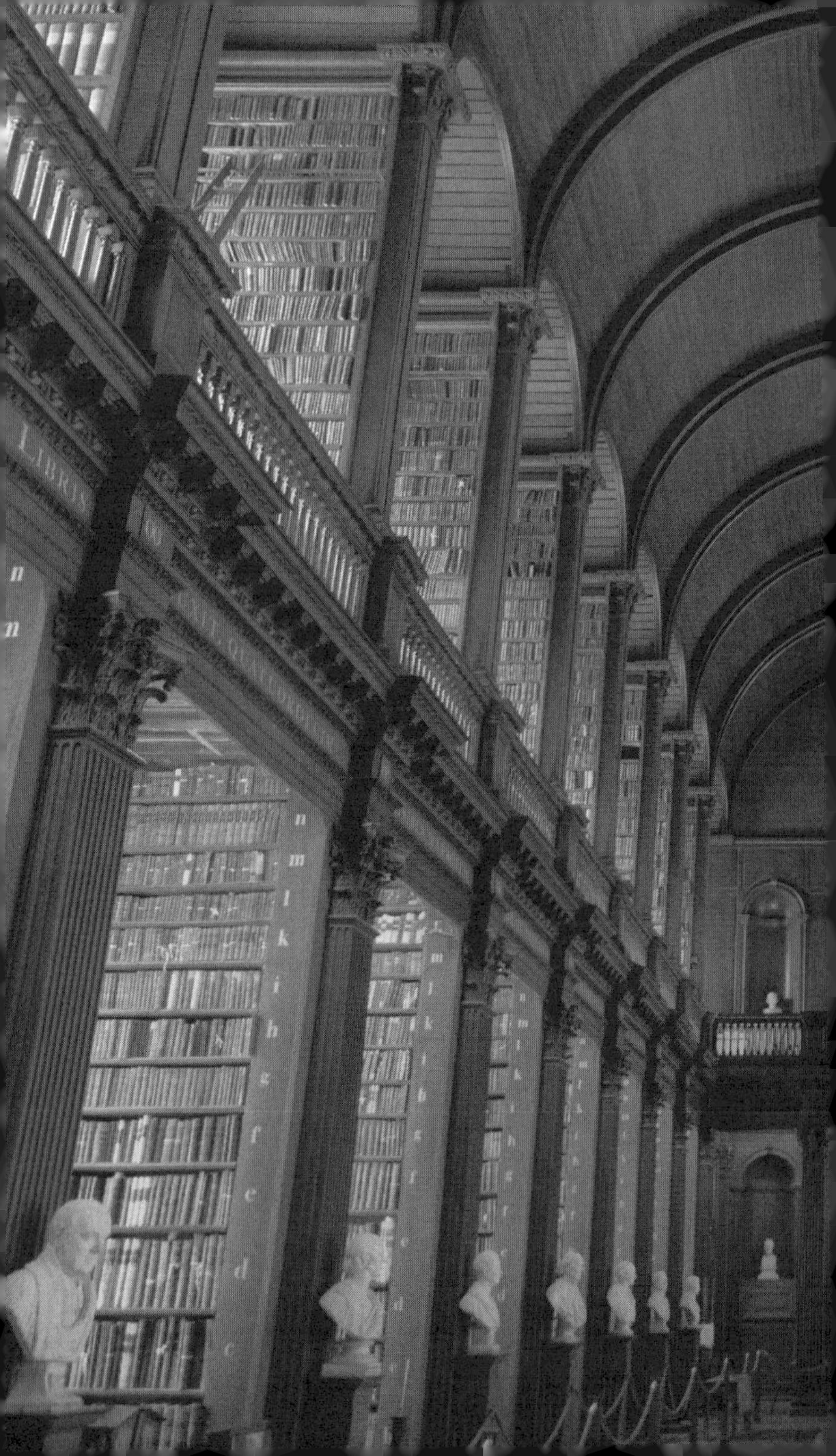

CHAPTER
FOUR

A scream rips from my throat and the ground underneath the pentagram shakes and buckles. The candle flames blaze higher. Tearing my gaze away from the hazy outline of the Horned God is impossible and as I watch, his smile widens.

There's a flash of white teeth in the dappled sunlight and that one expression chills me straight to the marrow of my bones.

All for you.

I swear it's his voice in my head instead of my own, and any sort of joy I'd felt in the vision, dancing around the bonfire, disappears under a swell of dread.

Magic thickens until I'm surprised no one is choking, their chants constant and low level compared to the throbbing heartbeat. We're living in an Edgar Allen Poe poem and I'm the only one who sees the truth.

"What do you want with me?" I stop screaming to ask the question, my throat raw.

The haze thickens until even the outline of the Horned God is hard to make out. He bows his head and the edges of his horns scrape the tree trunks.

Suddenly a boom rocks the ceremony and my magic reacts, erupting out of me and reaching for the Horned God. The witches holding my arms lose their grip, their balance, and freed, I surge to my feet. Fog winds through the trees, no longer stopped by our sacred circle.

No, not fog. *Smoke* and ash.

A second boom follows the first and this time I know exactly where it's coming from. What the sound really means. Turning, the burning edges of the ancient library are barely visible.

"Mom." Her name escapes before I realize what I've said and, as if conjured, she steps through the crowd seething and red-faced.

All eyes are on me and every single one of them are accusatory.

"Yasmine, what happened?" she barks out.

She grabs me by the shoulders and shakes me hard enough for my brain to crack.

"I didn't...I don't know!"

"This isn't the way things are supposed to go. You were fighting the High Priest. That's why the spell didn't work!" Her hands lift to her sides, put out, pissed off. "Not only were you fighting, you let your magic run away from you. Look what you did to the library!"

It seems we all know better than to try to extinguish

the flames. The roar, the heat, we feel and hear it from the clearing. It's too late; whatever backlash happened, the library will be gone in a matter of minutes.

Tears burn the corners of my eyes, racing down my cheeks in a bid for freedom. "I don't understand. It wasn't me. Mom, you have to believe me."

Jaw clenched, her expression promising retribution, Mom asks, "What don't you understand? You were supposed to let the ceremony take place and you fought it every step of the way. Your refusal led to your magic going haywire and now everything we love is destroyed."

Not everything, I want to say. My family is—My breath catches in my chest.

"Remi," I whisper.

I saw her run toward the library before the ceremony commenced. What if she was inside? What if she's hurt?

Mom's fingers dig into my flesh to keep me in place when I try to run.

The strange fog is gone as though it never existed in the first place and amid the crackling sound of hungry flames, the rest of the coven members shake their heads.

Lark grabs her cheeks, her face frozen in horror.

Mom is the only one still willing to look at me while the others groan, lifting hands to their faces to match Lark.

Wood and stone groan, the library structure more than likely succumbing to the flames, and with the efficiency of a timer going off, everyone drops their hands to their sides. Their faces clear and Lark is the first one to come to, to be freed from whatever had fogged their minds.

Like the blast woke them from some kind of trance.

"I'm not sure what's going on," one of them mutters, sounding disoriented.

The tears fall harder until I see Mom through a blur. On my twenty-first birthday, as the coven librarian's daughter, I'm supposed to ascend to the caste of Clerics as is my divine right. Instead, I'm failing, I'm hurting people, and I'm seeing things, while everyone else around me struggles to figure out exactly what's going on.

Mom takes me by the elbow and drags me out of the clearing. The cape loosely draped around my shoulders drops forgotten to the ground and I kick up dirt, not fully in control of my feet.

"This is an outrage," Mom mutters under her breath. "What did you *do*, Yasmine?"

It's on repeat, not only on her tongue but in my head.

What did I do?

What did I do?

I can hardly look at the smoldering library with bright blue and orange flames reaching up toward the clouds. Whatever blast took it out did quick work and the books inside, all those lovely books, all that knowledge, is gone.

We wait in the parking lot for the local police and fire departments to arrive to put out the flames, now that the coven has woken up.

Woken up from their trance only to point the finger

at me, and maybe it belongs there. Maybe I really did this. But my magic has never been strong enough to accomplish anything close, and fire is not my element.

Although the heat is enough to dry my tears, they keep falling, more and more in a desperate bid to escape my body. I would, too, if I was able.

Escape.

I want to be anywhere but here faced so completely with my failure. My thoughts attack me harsher and with more accuracy than any of Mom's questions, wanting to know how and why.

Why?

Eli materializes out of the confusion and works a little bit of magic. Something to keep the humans from seeing anything supernatural, a spell he's woven to confuse and obfuscate many times before, for the magic hidden here. Outsiders aren't welcomed in our sacred circles but the community is already involved. We need their help.

To them, this is our family home.

To our coven, it was our history and our lineage.

More firetrucks rush into the driveway with a buzz of sound and sirens, hoses at the ready.

It takes them way too long to extinguish the last of the flames. All that's left is a charred husk of everything I love. It's the only home I've known and the world I've wrapped around my shoulders like a safety blanket since Mom found out I have magic.

Home is gone now. Everything is gone.

The library and my future and my ascension. I don't need to be told to understand the grim reality of the circumstances and what I'll face once the mele has calmed.

Once the last police cruiser leaves the lot, there are only the three of us: me, Mom, and Eli.

Eli turns to me and the disappointment rolling off him makes me want to start with the excuses, like I can somehow convince him of my innocence and how this is a mistake. I never meant for my magic to erupt the way it did, in relation to the Horned God, but I also didn't do this.

He sighs. "I'm not sure what we're going to do from here." Tall and slender, he looms over me with a fuzzy top of bright blond and silver hair on his head. His eyes stand out in a pale shade of blue and right now they bore through me.

"The coven is going to have to investigate this." His attention remains on me. "At this point, the culprit of the library's destruction seems clear. Now, I'm not willing to say this was done intentionally, Yasmine, we're going to have to see what comes up. I'm simply telling you, telling you both—" his gaze flicks to Mom. "This does not look good."

Me. All fingers definitely point to me and there's nothing I can do to dissuade their assumption, either. Everything I want to say will come across as hollow and flimsy excuses.

I must have done it. Right? Starting with the strange book I had known better than to open.

Another week goes by before Mom even decides it necessary to speak to me or make eye contact. We move into the coven house in one of the empty rooms, and sharing a bedroom with my mom is much harder when she's zip lipped.

I'm not sure what's worse, her condemnation or her silence. I try to live with it, walking on eggshells while the coven makes their decision about me.

She won't tell me about Remi, either. I've tried asking, to see what happened to my sister who is nowhere to be seen, only to have Mom turn on her heel and leave the room, as though she can't bear to be around me. No one will tell me what happened to my sister.

Mom won't listen to me.

She didn't a week ago when I wanted to tell her about the vision, and she refuses to now.

Finally, we're called in front of them.

A kind woman with wrinkles around her eyes knocks on our door and exchanges a long, loaded look with Mom. She finally sighs and nods, the other woman retreating until it's only the two of us again.

We walk down the hallway together in sullen silence.

It feels like an eternity. The ache in my chest deepens until each breath is a struggle and my feet weigh as much as anchors.

Two witches wait at the door to the ritual room to greet us with bowed heads, Mom keeping ahead of me. Eli stands in the center of the room with Lark at his side. Both of them wear matching robes and equally disdainful expressions.

They've already made their decision. This meeting… it's to hand out judgment. Once we've arrived, a clap of magic heralds the start of the meeting and my legs turn to jelly.

"We've been called here today for a serious discussion, a matter most grave. That of our esteemed librarian's daughter, Yasmine, and her willful destruction of our coven's most precious knowledge," Eli starts gravely.

I gawk at the man.

Me?

He really thinks I have the power to do something so horrible to a place I love?

I open my mouth to defend myself only to hear Mom hiss at me to be quiet.

"Her mother, Jaime Williams, has released her daughter into the custody of the High Priestess and myself, as is her right in this case," he continues. "In order to properly mete out justice in this matter."

It's the first I'm hearing about this.

My head spins and I turn to Mom with stars and black dots dancing in front of my vision. "What? What is he saying?" I ask, my words thick.

When had she done that?

"I'm an adult. I-I'm twenty-one. You can't just give me away like that." I want to reach out for her and something stops me.

Mom stands stoically with her attention on our Priest and Priestess without even a sideways glance for me.

"I declare," Eli intones, "before our coven, that as our ward, Yasmine Williams must be sent to the Andora Academy for Witchcraft to learn not only their ways but more about her magic. She is a danger to herself and others unless she learns mastery. We cannot allow her to remain unchecked."

A rock plummets to the bottom of my stomach and further south. The Andora Academy for Witchcraft? What the hell is that?

"Mom? I don't understand," I hiss out. "They're sending me away?"

She still refuses to look and there's deep knowing inside of me that says I'll never have her attention again.

Even when I should be an adult in charge of myself, I've been given up. Sentenced to be sent away to some place I've never heard about.

A sick heat rises from my gut and my throat closes, cutting off anything else I might have said.

"What about Remi?" I ask. "I need to know if Remi is okay before I leave. Let me see her. Please?"

I have to see her. These people, the coven members I've always felt at home among, have turned their back on me, but they should at least tell me what happened to my sister.

"The fate of your family is no concern of yours any longer," the High Priest tells me. There isn't a hint of kindness in his voice and his words are an anchor dragging me down so far into bleak and horrible feelings, I'm not sure how long it will take me to get back to myself.

"You used magic that threatened us all." Lark, usually so soft spoken and kind, the embodiment of the mother energy, bites out her words. I feel them in my marrow like ice-cold shackles. "You fought the ceremony and brought darkness to us."

"Until such time as she is sent to the academy, she shall be shunned," Eli finishes. "Yasmine is ousted from her place within the coven. As it is decreed…"

"So mote it be," the rest of the room says as one. There, I realize numbly. There is the drop of the ax I've been waiting for, and it's as swift and deadly as I imagined.

CHAPTER
FIVE

The rest of my days in the mortal world pass in a blur.

I have very little stuff to move, so when Lark escorts me to a chamber on the other side of the ritual room, it's basically only me and the bed. The dresser stays practically empty except for a few essentials, mocking, and the small window is set so high up on the wall so as not to allow me any kind of view. Chamber, right. It's a cell, while they wait for the arrangements to be made at Andora.

Eventually, several of the other members bring in changes of clothes they must have purchased for me, along with a few items saved from the fire. Things I cling to when night falls and I'm too tired to cry into my pillow.

There's the book, with my hero in the Scottish Highlands. There's a framed picture of me and Remi from her tenth birthday where she'd pushed my face into her cake once she blew out the candles.

It's just enough to fill a suitcase and, although the clothes aren't mine, whoever brought them did a good job of nailing my aesthetic.

Old lady chic.

It's more than I deserve considering what I did to the library.

The more time passes, the more I convince myself it's true—the first was my fault.

I take care of myself, I feed myself. I'm isolated. When I'm sick of my own company, I head to the living room, and no one I pass in the hall acknowledges my existence.

I've cried myself to sleep so many times my eyes are permanently swollen and I've got nothing left inside of me.

The days tick down, however, and by the end of the week it's time for me to leave for the academy.

I stare at the suitcase on the bed, too exhausted to even start to worry what it will be like there. October… I've missed the first part of the semester, coming in just a little before halfway.

"What can they possibly teach me that Mom didn't cover?" I ask out loud, if only for the sound of a voice. I flick the zipper on the side of the case. "Not like I even know where I'm going. I've never had a chance to research it, either."

No one has told me anything about the place and I've been cut off from access to books. Like I'll somehow use them for kindling or something equally destructive.

I drag the zipper closed and shut away any link to my old life.

I get that the coven is trying to be cautious, I really do. And under normal circumstances I might have mustered a little excitement for an adventure. Something completely outside of the future I'd been prepared for my whole life.

Going to an actual magical school will give me a chance to hone my skills further and to make friends. Besides my sister and my familiar, I've never had friends before. My life is too isolated.

These aren't normal circumstances though. They are utterly *ab*normal. This is different.

I roll the suitcase down the hall to the front porch and the waiting car.

The woman in the driver's seat, the one who doesn't move to help me stow my suitcase, is a stranger wearing Mom's face. She keeps her gaze on the road and her hands stiff on the wheel. She's allowed to take me to the academy.

She's allowed to say goodbye.

Anything other than those two simple things are against the coven's rules for this situation. Except those things aren't simple?

I tap my foot on the floorboard, up and down, leg bobbing with uncontrollable movement. I want to point out the beautiful day and the clear blue sky overhead. I want to talk to Mom about the leaves changing and what kinds of trees have the best color this year.

I want to ask her if she's sure I'm the one who was

supposed to ascend to Cleric or if a mistake might have been made somewhere along the way?

I say none of those things and a glance at myself in the rearview mirror shows me paler than usual. Tight lipped and tense while the miles tick down.

I've got a lump in my throat the size of Texas and about as much excitement as facing a week alone in the Sahara with no food or water.

The drive takes hours, during which Mom doesn't slow the car from a steady pace. Out of town, out of the next one, until we're so far outside of my comfort zone I recognize nothing.

The hills roll slightly here, and clumps of trees break up the landscape. It's what people in fiction call *pastoral*. It's lovely to finally see but I wish Remi was here to tease me, or Mom would put one of her Hindi songs on blast and make us scream the words with her.

We finally arrive at Andora Academy, noticeable only by the thick iron gates stretching along the hills and through the trees.

Mom parks the car just outside of the looming fence and silently walks with me to the front gates.

The intricate iron design on the metal catches my attention. Especially when the gates open on their own and give me a glimpse into a wide courtyard of endless green grass.

Towering trees mark the landscape of the campus as well, thicker and more gnarled than anything we'd seen on our drive. Their leaves are a perpetual green against the golden tones of the outside world and through the gate, through the trees, I catch a glimpse of stone roofs.

Throat dry, eyes drier, I stop at the gate and turn to face Mom for what I hope isn't the last time.

Do I thank her for the drive? Am I allowed to say anything at all or is it better if I keep a stiff upper lip and walk off without looking back to her?

I have no clue how to operate or what's expected of me.

Dropped into a strange world.

We square off from each other, too tense, both waiting for the other to bend or break.

"Make the most of your time here, Yas," Mom says in a low voice. "This is a good school. You'll learn a lot."

"Is that what they told you to tell me?" I mutter.

She ducks and a lock of hair falls free from her bun. Even without the library to helm, she's wearing her hair the same way. Only now it's messy, frizzy, and there are dark circles underneath her eyes.

"Andora Academy is the premier magical academy in this area. If you'd been anyone else, you would have come here with the others in your class," she continues.

"Good to know." She's going to make me cry again, just when I thought I'd be okay.

"Your family will try to fix this," she replies. "Whatever it is."

She's not supposed to talk to me like this, but I guess this can fall under the header of *goodbye*.

Unsure what to say, I nod along with her words. I'll do whatever it takes to make it count while I'm here but the longer we stand, the more my nerves grow heavy and start to fray. A weight presses down on every part of my body and turns me to lead. This isn't right.

This isn't how things are supposed to go.

And how can I be sure the Horned God won't find me here?

I only felt a strange pulse of energy once during my stay at the coven house. Once, in the dead of night after my tears stopped and I lay on my back listening to the hush of my breathing.

The moonlight sifted through the high window of the chamber and although there was nothing to block the view, I saw a flicker. A shadow darker than the night itself and gone as quickly as it appeared.

"Remi's okay."

I barely hear Mom's whisper and might have missed it if I hadn't been staring right at her mouth.

Remi...

"Oh my god." The words burst out of me.

She's fine; thankfully, she's fine.

Mom's eyes dart left to right and narrow in a silent warning for me to drop it. To not make a big deal or say anything else, to not ask more questions. Clearly, Mom isn't supposed to reveal anything about Remi to me. Any nerves I felt are buried under the relief at knowing I didn't lose my sister.

"Can you tell me anything more?" I press. "Please, Mom. What happened to her? Where is she? Is she really fine?"

Mom huffs out a breath, once again checking to make sure there is no one close enough to overhear before leaning close and saying under her breath, "I had time to think, to see. I know your magic isn't harmful, Yas. I'm going to do whatever it takes to prove it to the coven. We just have to play along and give me the time I need."

I have to crane my head closer to make out what she's saying. Not even a whisper, only the smallest movement of her mouth, but I understand, and shiver.

Thank you.

I mouth the words.

Mom believes me. It's more than I can ask for.

"Until I figure this out, you need to learn all that you've not been able to learn from your home studies. Do you understand?" she asks.

I nod.

"And above all, don't talk about the ascension." Mom looks up sharply, making sure we're still alone. "Don't tell anyone I'm a Cleric or that you will become one too. Okay? It's exceedingly important."

"I won't say a word," I breathe.

Mom does a great job of making the smallest things in life of utmost importance. Now, however, she's pale. Serious. She doesn't need to impress how imperative it is not to speak of what I'm about to become.

It's our secret.

Mom straightens and clears her throat. "You're going to be fine," she assures me in a louder tone. "Keep your nose out of trouble and study hard."

I want to reach out and hug her, to feel her arms around me and know when she tells me I'm going to be fine, it's the truth. Instead, Mom takes a step in the opposite direction and stares at me from top to bottom. A sharp nod shows she's okay with her assessment, whatever it is.

"Mom." The wind steals my voice.

She's not crying, and I won't either. I'll settle for a smile if I can't have the hug.

This is our so-called heartfelt goodbye. And my entry into my new world. Mom has never been overly emotional about anything that I've seen, and she is not now that I'm being taken away.

Did I expect anything else?

She hustles back to the car without a look over her shoulder. I stand rooted to the spot until her car disappears from sight and I'm left with only my pounding pulse and the wind in my ears.

It's not really the greatest combination.

One thing Mom never counted on me realizing: I read between the lines and I know, as someone banished from the coven, this goodbye is our last. I'll be unable to have any further communication with Mom, with Remi.

I've never been truly alone before.

There's a first time for everything but this is not a gentle transition; it's a shove out of the nest in the most violent way.

The wind takes on a biting quality and seeps beneath my skin as the sun dips behind a cloud. Alone, and lost, and expected to do great things.

Even exiled, there are expectations.

Right then, I let myself have a moment to grieve for everything I've lost along with my terror of the unknown, especially when I'm not sure if I'll ever be able to get it back again.

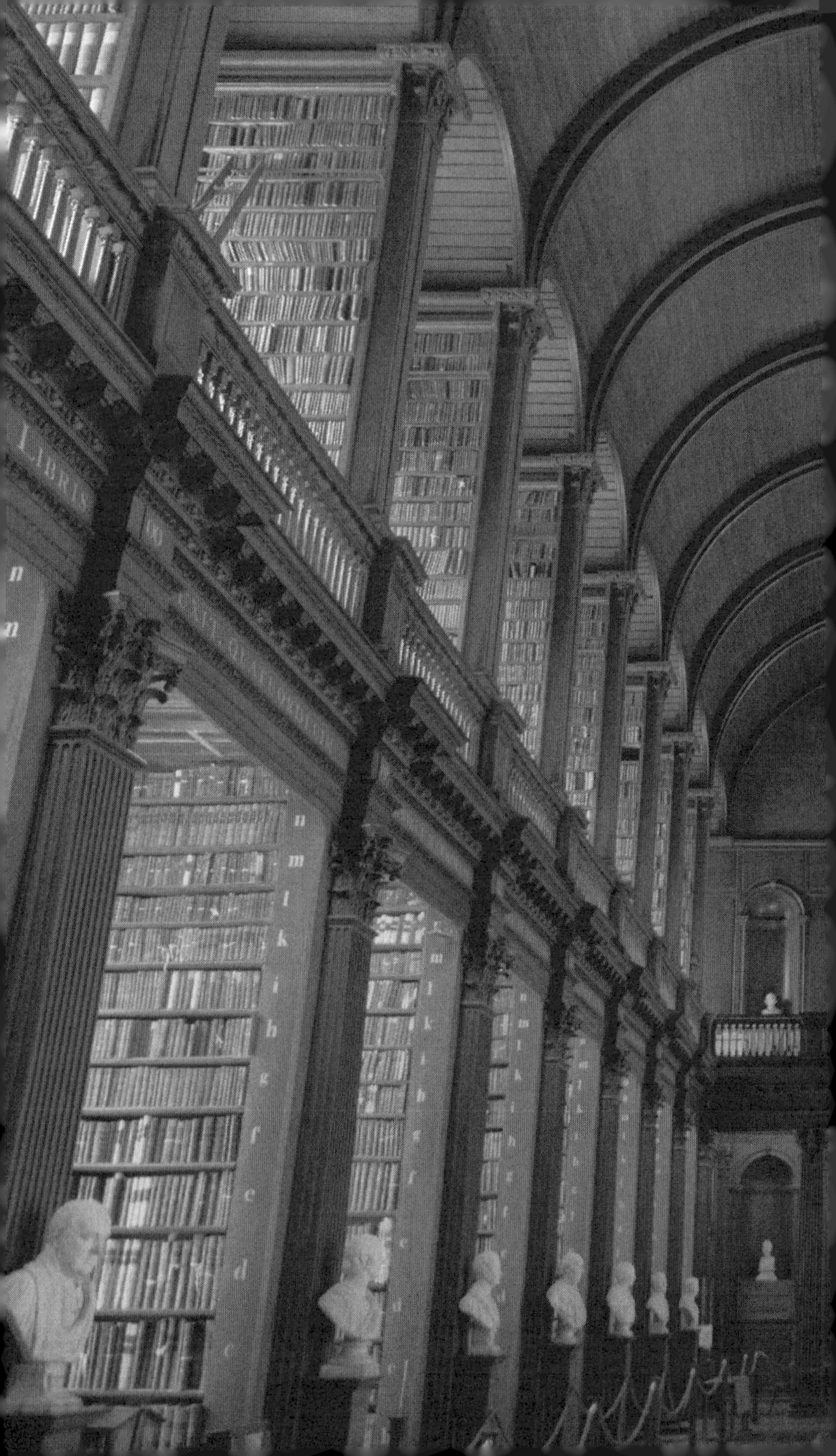

CHAPTER SIX

I stand outside the gates for a long moment, holding my breath.

It's only the beating of my heart and the wind tickling the soft hairs around my face. No shadows and no fog. There's no ticking heartbeat counting down to an explosion.

The heartbeat that ruined my life.

When nothing happens, I turn to face the open gates waiting for me to step onto academy grounds, and I run face first into a wall of muscle.

I freeze, hand automatically lifting to shield myself from the wrath of the Horned God. He's found me. Even here, so far away from my hometown, he's found me.

I open my mouth to shout when a male voice cuts through my fear.

"Miss Yasmine Williams?" The security guard wears black and gold with a cap set at an angle on top of his head. "We've been expecting you. Welcome to Andora

Academy. The headmaster sent me to escort you onto campus."

He's not tall enough to be the Horned God, yet I wince. Flinch. Even knowing logically I'm staring at a flesh-and-blood man and not a phantom, I react.

"Oh, hi. Thank you. Nice to meet you, Officer…" I trail off and search the front of his shirt for something with his name on it. "Anthony."

He's one of the few mortals I've ever met besides Remi's friends and her boyfriend.

"You're on time, which is always appreciated. I'm sure you're anxious to get started as well. You've missed quite a bit of the semester, but I know I speak for everyone when I say we're always happy to have new students," Officer Anthony says.

If he notices my freeze reaction, he doesn't mention it.

He flashes me the ghost of a smile and gestures with his nose toward his hand, his fingers already clenched around my suitcase.

I don't remember seeing Mom drop it off.

Everything I have, in one piece of luggage. Funny thing is that I'm not even upset about it. The relief at knowing Remi is fine, the fear of what's waiting for me on the other side of the iron fence…those are much more pressing issues.

Officer Anthony clears his throat and jerks his head to the still open gate. "Let's go," he urges. "It's time to get you registered. The sooner you're settled, the sooner you can start making friends."

He leads the way, not minding how I dawdle,

gawking at the fence. It's higher than I originally thought, the peaks at the top of the ornate design spearing into the sky.

This place is strange. Do they need such a heavy-duty fence to keep their students inside? Or to keep the outside world at bay?

Once we're through, the gates clang closed on their own with a finality I feel inside of me. Well, I'm here. The world hasn't crashed and there are no more magical oddities happening. If anything, the campus is a little slice of heaven, the rest of the world fading away as it spreads out in front of me. Several tall, Gothic structures take up space intermittently on the lawn.

"Andora is one of the most respected magical academies," Officer Anthony is saying. "I'm mortal but my family has strong ties to the founding members who started this school, and I've been lucky enough to find employment here."

"You like it?" I ask.

"Great place to work," he agrees without hesitation. "Rarely have I heard anyone complain about the school, either. I'm sure you're going to like it here."

He doesn't know my circumstances. He's making bold claims for a mortal. Since I want him to be right, desperately, I nod and do my best to listen to him as he talks me through our walk.

The building closest to me has dual towers of black brick with darker shingles. It's heavy, oppressive, something like the huntsman's cottage in a twisted fairy tale.

The officer's strides are much longer than my own

short legs and with my gawking, I struggle to keep up with him.

Ancient trees decorate the space between buildings, and the foliage casts shadows on the ground that seem to move on their own. Through it all are cobblestone paths and students hustling from building to building.

Classes must have just let out.

This place is larger than anything Remi has told me about human high schools. Having never been to one of them or to a college myself, I can't say for sure, but I'm going to need a map.

Officer Anthony chuckles at whatever expression he sees when he glances at me.

"It's all a little new for you, isn't it?" he asks, not unkindly.

I gulp, nod again, and say, "I've never been out of my small town."

"We get a lot of that here."

The student body is more diverse than I would have imagined for all of us being witches. The others are lost in their own little worlds, groups of two, three, four people walking the paths and laughing among themselves. All dressed the same.

Only a handful of them bother to look at me and my escort.

Officer Anthony calls my name and I have to peel my attention away from the campus. Several of the buildings are more than one story as well. How many students attend the academy? Hopefully someone will be able to answer these things for me once I'm registered.

"It's right over here," he assures me. "Not much further now, Miss Williams."

He heads toward one of the low-level buildings at the end of the great lawn, with massive cathedral windows and a door that looks like it weighs about two thousand pounds. The handles on each of the doors are solid gold with curling ivy designs on the hammered edges.

"If you have any questions at all, feel free to reach out to me or one of my guys," Officer Anthony says. He drops me off at those doors with a salute, handing me the suitcase handle. "We're pretty friendly here. Welcome home."

Home.

I'm holding my breath again. Something I don't realize until the black dots are back in front of my eyes.

I'm not sure I'll ever be home again but this is where I am for the moment, and Mom wants me to work hard. To study harder. I'll make her proud and hopefully somewhere along the line, the coven will decide I'm really not to blame for the library.

A girl can hope.

Inside, I stop in front of the glass partition keeping the lobby separated from the offices to the left.

I knock against the glass to get the attention of the clerk and smile. She frowns at me, forcing me to reassess the smile. "Hello. I'm Yasmine Williams. I'm supposed to get registered today?"

"Yasmine, Yasmine…" the front desk clerk looks like a quintessential grandma figure with a white bun and dark horn-rimmed glasses over lined eyes. "Yes, you're right on time. Your High Priest, Elijah, confirmed your status with us. We're happy to have you. Here you go."

She grabs a folder from the desk and holds it out to me. "You've got your housing assignment there. Of course, your list of courses are all laid out as well," she continues. "I'm sure you're eager to get started and catch up with your peers, but according to what we've heard, you'll have no problems. Your High Priest described you as bright and inquisitive."

Too fast.

It's all happening too fast.

"You arrived late for the semester's beginning but we're hopeful you'll have every opportunity to adjust," she says and smiles, but it doesn't look genuine.

I do my best to return it for real this time and fail miserably. Her eyes radiate a sort of soft sympathy and I wonder if she's been made aware of my entire situation, not just the things Eli said to make her more inclined to accept me.

If she has any idea what the coven says I've done, will she take her smile back?

"Thank you," I reply. "I appreciate your help."

"You'll find everything you need in the packet, okay sweetie?" she continues. "And if you have any other questions then please don't hesitate to let me know. There is always someone behind the desk." She reaches out of the small opening in the glass front and points to the door. "You see the building with the copper weathervane? It's down the winding path a ways but the weathervane stands out. That's where you'll find your resident adviser, on the second floor in room

206. She'll get you checked into your dorm with the others."

Checked in.

Everything is in the packet.

My thoughts spiral and the rest of me is weighed down and ready to sink into the floor.

I thank her again, clutching the packet to my chest.

The sun is way too bright when I step outside, tickling my skin and tugging hair loose from my ponytail. *Take a beat.* I have to stop for a breath, a moment to myself before I have to dive into life in this place.

What is it going to be like to have a roommate? And why doesn't the resident adviser live in the dorm with me? Maybe she handles all first years. I have no idea how these things work.

I've been specially trained since birth to step into the cast of Clerics, which leaves me little better than a hermit in this case. I have no idea how to react. This is so outside of my scope it's enough to give me palpitations.

Except I'm wasting time.

White knuckled, I lug my suitcase into the dorm building with the copper weathervane on top. The front door is painted yellow and stands out against the black shingles and shutters. One of the taller buildings, too. I find my Resident Advisor on floor two, exactly where the woman in the registration office told me she would be.

Amy.

She squeals when she sees me and wraps her arms

around my shoulders with enough force to make me drop my luggage.

"I know I speak for everyone when I say we're really happy to have you, Yasmine," she says against my ear. "You're going to love it here."

"So everyone keeps telling me," I reply.

She slings her arm over my shoulder like we're best friends. "It's true, though. It's basically a fairytale. Where are you from? Why are you so late in the semester?"

What might have been nice is being briefed on the ride here, not on what to keep secret, but on what lies to say instead.

I offer Amy a few flimsy pieces of information which she seems to accept.

"It seems to me like you're starting over," she says. "And in my personal opinion, this is the best place to start over. People here are sweet and really sympathetic. A lot of other students have come from pretty bad backgrounds, too."

Several things stand out immediately about Amy: she's perky and forever optimistic. She's the kind of person who can find the silver lining no matter how bleak the situation.

Her black hair is cut short and sharp around her chin. Sky-blue eyes dominate her face, and her lips are a cupid's bow slicked with something shiny. "The dorms are assigned based on a witch's top five talents and strengths," she tells me, beckoning me into her room. "There's no separation by years, only skills. Where your strengths lie and whatnot. As such, you've been sent to live in a dorm with others like you."

With nowhere else to go, I follow her inside and she points to her bed. Flower print in bright pastel colors.

I should have guessed.

I gingerly sit on a corner of her mattress as she continues with, "The hope is that, by grouping young witches together, their talents will grow. You should try to make friends. You know, among the other students like you."

"I'm not even sure what my talents are," I say, squirming. "This is all super new to me."

And I have to be as bland as possible. Amy seems like a really nice person but trusting her is a mistake.

Trusting anyone, at this point, is a mistake.

"You'll learn." She sounds so sure. "There are five main houses on campus. Otherwise known as ADZEX." She says the acronym as one singular word and with a sing-song tone. Then proceeds to tick them off on her fingers. "There's Alchemy and Astrology. Divination. Zeitgeist. Elementa, and Unknown."

Said fingers wiggle on the last word. The mystery dorm for the misfits who don't fit in, I take it.

"They're all based on occult terms. You see?" she says with a toothy smile. "Unknown is symbolized by an X. There aren't as many students there as you might think so it's one of the smaller residences on campus."

"That's where I'm going. Isn't it?" I haven't even looked at my paperwork yet.

Amy nods. "Since you haven't been tested then that's

where you'll go until you are. Come on. I'll show you the way."

I blink at her. "Is this place one of the dorms?" I ask.

"No, no, this is where the staff stay. I'm the resident adviser so I need my own place for things along with the rest of us. There aren't many but half of the building is used for offices and the other residences! You dig?" The finger wiggling stays in place. "Grab your suitcase, Yas. You don't mind if I call you *Yas*, do you? I'll show you where you're going to be staying."

I follow her out into the open air like a lost puppy with my feet aching from all the walking I've done around campus already.

"Usually the testing takes place on the first day, right after registration. I'm sure they'll have you scheduled in the next week or so. If you don't hear anything, then let me know and I'll get it set up for you." Amy continues to point out each of the lovely buildings along the way to my dorm. Her chipper voice is the perfect cadence for storytelling. Especially to children. She doesn't look like a witch, either. She looks like she belongs in a kid show talking to puppets or something.

"This is your dorm." Amy holds her arms out wide to the single-story saltbox with moss covered shingles. It stands out among the other buildings because it looks more old-Salem than Gothic. The misfit students in the misfit house, I think to myself, staring at the shutters on the windows to the left of the door, swaying slightly in the wind.

The place is longer than it is wide, too. A walk around the side shows the building being added on to repeatedly, to accommodate more people if I have to guess.

I wonder if it's a choice the school made or if this building was the first one built on campus. It certainly looks its age.

Creaking hinges included.

A large elm tree shades the entrance and moss grows on the shingles, all of the plants in the front garden adapted to the lack of sunlight. Under the right circumstances it might even be cute.

Amy stares appraisingly at the house with her hands on her hips. "Don't let X House worry you too much. The houses and their classifications aren't really important right now. Trust me."

She sounds assuring.

I have to wonder if it's all an act or if she really feels this optimistic about everything. She's obviously been chosen for her position for a reason.

From where I'm standing, this is the house for outcasts and the people who even a school for witches can't seem to place. The ones who don't belong in any boxes.

The house doesn't have the same lovely trappings as the other buildings on campus and not because it's a bit rundown. Everything about it is unique. Which is a nice word for unkempt.

They've placed me with the people who don't belong and a part of me knows they're right.

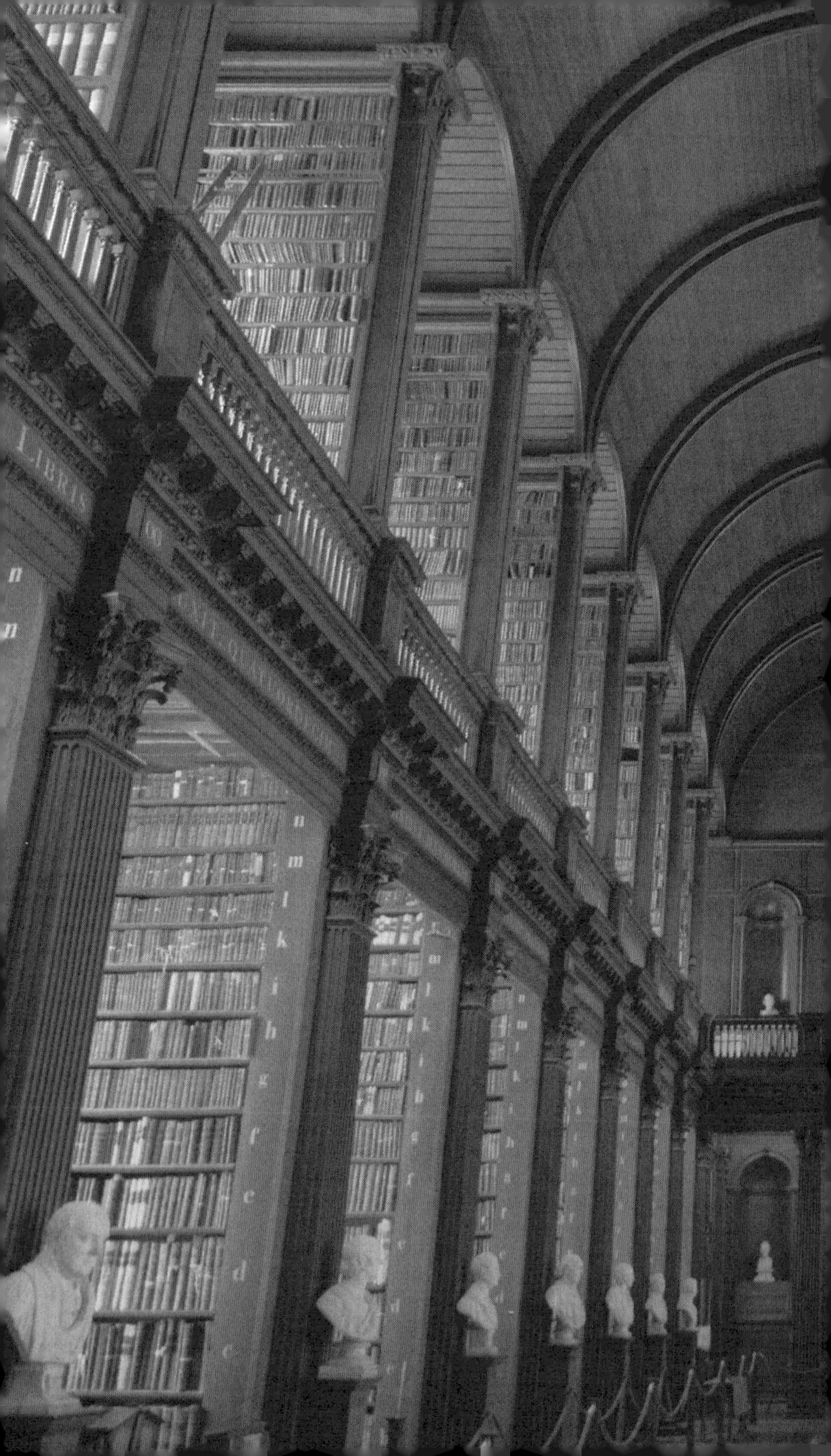

CHAPTER
SEVEN

"X House," I say out loud.

Amy flashes me a huge white smile. "I think once you settle in you'll find it more than adequate. At least, until you get your magic tested."

"And what if I test and I'm still in X House?" I ask. The way she makes it sound is that I'll surely be moved soon.

I've never felt more confused.

I might have missed her slight twitch. "It will all work itself out," she replies as a non-answer.

The other part of me, the one who has always struggled to feel comfortable with my place in life, wonders what other talents I might have that haven't been tapped into yet. Mental fingers crossed I have more talents than I've managed to manifest in my Cleric training. I'm good for books and for short blasts of magic, good for ascending to the next level, but what if those things aren't enough to keep me here?

Why do I even want to stay?

I'm curious why Mom doesn't want me to reveal we're Clerics.

Since Amy seems to have settled in for more of our introductory conversation, I decide to ask her. As cautiously as possible, of course.

"What about Clerics?" I want to know. "Like, in general."

Amy shoots me some serious side eye. "What do you mean?" she asks with equal caution.

"I mean, what house do Clerics fit into? Shouldn't they have their own place on campus?"

She shakes her head, the confusion seeping from her expression to be replaced with her usual bright cheer. "I get why you'd be curious because of the founders of this place."

The what?

"Yasmine, Clerics haven't been around for over one hundred and fifty years. You're crazy!" She breaks off in a giggle. "The last Cleric was executed at the stake for treason. The whole subject is a bit taboo, if you know what I mean."

My blood runs cold and my jaw drops open. "You're kidding me," I hear myself say from a distance.

"Looks like you're going to have a bit of history to catch up on. Don't worry, it's not a bad thing. A lot of students who come here for their first semester aren't really *up* on our history, if you know what I mean. They've heard their fair share of gossip, but they don't know the real story. Oh! Here." Amy digs around in her pocket. "Hold out your hand."

Stiffly, obediently, I do as she says.

"Here is your key to your room." She places a slender gold filigree key, as short as my pinky finger, on my open palm. "And the entry code to the dorm is the Fibonacci sequence, so it's easy to remember." She makes a little shooing motion with her hands.

Had I freaked her out with my question about Clerics?

So many questions, all of them swimming around my head. Because Clerics clearly exist…I'm here, and my mom.

"You're not going to come inside with me?" I ask Amy.

Amy continues to giggle and steps back until she's standing in the single sunspot on the lawn, shielding her eyes from the glow above. "No, hun, this is where we part ways. But you know where to find me if you have any more questions. Everything you need to know is going to be included in whatever file Gladys gave you when you registered. Take care!"

Amy waves a vigorous goodbye and leaves me standing a few paces away from the raised stoop of the front porch. *It's time.* There's no reason for me to be nervous putting in the keycode. No reason to be nervous as I step into the front entry hall, distracted by what she'd said.

The last Cleric had been executed for treason, but Eli or Lark never made mention of it. All my life I've heard about the honor of the Clerics and how we are important to our covens for keeping the balance.

Finding that damn book changed things for me.

I find the way to my room, which is catty-corner to

one of the bathrooms. Loud and stinky. Already the sound of running water from the showers is painfully clear through the thin walls.

The dorm is co-ed as well. Which I discover when a half-naked dude wrapped in an old blue towel steps out of said bathroom and barks at me to get out of his way. He flings a bit of water my way as he steps past.

Well, this is going to be interesting.

I do my best to not stare after him, to not blush the way my body seems determined to do.

Considering how I've never had to truly deal with the opposite sex before, I don't want to act as ignorant as I am. Up until this point, I've gotten my info from Remi and her boyfriend, or from the romance novels she's slipped me.

And the guy in the towel looks nothing like Seamus in his kilt so I'm a fish out of water here.

I peel my eyes to the door, tugging on my suitcase, and finally enter the room beside the bathroom.

"Hello?" I call out. "Any roomies home?"

The room opens up into a typical square with two beds, two dressers, and two desks. What I'm not expecting is the boy-band posters splattered on every available wall space. Or the way my roommate has clearly taken over the entirety of the space. There is nothing left for me here, nothing that I can make my own except for the twin mattress.

"If you need any help—"

The voice sounds directly next to my ear and although I recognize it, in a second, as Amy's, she still freaks me out. I jump off the ground and whirl around to face her with my heart racing and a hand pressed to my chest.

"I thought you left!" I slap a hand to my rapidly beating heart.

She shrugs, smiling. "I forgot to give you my cell number and let you know I'm personally available if you want to chat. I remember how it was when I first enrolled. Sometimes it's not as easy as we hope."

Amy gestures toward the room.

"Sometimes there's a lot of patchouli," she finishes.

My roommate isn't there, and I'm happy she isn't, to see me have a near heart attack.

"Thanks," I manage to say to Amy. I pocket the number she'd written on a slip of paper. "I appreciate your offer." Will I actually text her?

Her smile shifts into sympathetic territory. "You'll adjust. I'm sure of it."

Then I'm alone. Really, truly alone, with a thousand boy bands from the nineties staring at me from their decorated spots on the walls.

It's only me and my suitcase in the bubblegum pop room, the color combinations garish enough to make me a little queasy. The eyes on the posters track my movements as I flop down on the bare mattress and let my luggage topple to the floor with a clatter.

I'm here. Now what?

I'm here, and it's the last place I ever thought I'd be, the direction of my life changed irrevocably.

The decor is overwhelming, the small space overloaded with so many things from the human world that I'm not familiar with, and my mind burns with questions. My roommate must be a bit of a hoarder as her side of the room has every available space chock filled to bursting with personal items.

Taking a deep breath, I drop my head between my knees and focus on drawing an inhale to the count of four, holding it for five, exhaling for six.

The Clerics are gone.

How is it possible?

Are we the only ones left, anywhere?

Are we hiding for a reason?

I focus on breathing until I lose count because I definitely don't feel better. Like, not even a little bit.

And even the dresser that's supposed to be mine is covered with trinkets. It's the one closest to my bed so it's mine now. I'm going to have to ask my roommate about it, whenever she gets in.

Deciding to force myself to feel more positive, to steal a little bit of Amy's optimism, I grab the suitcase and set it next to me on the mattress, unzipping it.

And I screech again when my familiar pops out. "Gus!" My heart turns over in my chest. I can only look at him, to see for myself he really did survive the blast. He's whole.

Not that I thought he hadn't survived.

I would have known he'd died, the connection between us gone and the space in my head he's always occupied empty.

Still, he'd kept his distance while I lived in the coven house.

There I go, practically sobbing again. "I've never

been so happy to see you in my life! What are you doing here?"

He scurries up my arm, his voice in my head in such familiar soothing tones I'm a second away from losing it entirely.

I thought you'd need me, so I came. Like you were going to go away to academy without me? It's bad enough the wards at the coven house keep familiars on the outskirts.

I snuggle him close. "You're a lifesaver. I'm so glad you're here. I didn't even feel you there. I pause for a second. Their wards are that strong?"

Apparently so, and Gus does not sound happy about it.

There's no way I'm letting go of him, no way I want any more distance between us.

The mental connection between us is also a lifesaver, soothing the frayed edges of my mind like nothing else. Soon even my frantic wonderings about the Clerics take a backseat to the joy, the sheer relief, of having Gus nearby.

As my familiar, he is able to talk to me, and his side of the conversation is never relayed out loud. It's another level of bonding between us and something special we share.

And now, I'm not alone anymore.

Gus nestles against my chest and it's the most effective soothing mechanism I've ever experienced. His weight, his scent, his voice in my head, it's everything I need to tether me to my past. It's comfortable.

There is something shady going on, he tells me.

"That's a mouthful and you aren't even speaking

through your mouth. You know they sent me here because they think I burned the library."

Gus brushes his nose against my finger. *Not you, Yas. Something powerful, with enough magic to make the others think it was you. To point the blame in your direction.*

"You mean the—"

I break off when the door to the room slams open and crashes against the wall.

A fabulously dressed young woman stands in the doorway for a long moment, pausing for effect, before entering the room. She's done up in layers of pink with her hair in ombre pigtails. Yes, also pink. Her plaid school uniform has been adjusted, or transformed, to fit whatever rebellious attitude made her choose her current aesthetic.

Her gaze lands on me and, surprisingly, her features twist in a grin. "I knew I was getting a new roomie, but I thought you'd be in later! No idea why I thought that. Otherwise I would have cleaned up a bit. I'm really happy to have you here. It's been a long time since I had a roommate. Like, weeks." She twists a lock of hair around her finger, her nail polish matching the color of the strands.

She lacks the persona of Amy, the outright cheerleader kind of bubbly, but there's something real about her. Something with a little more depth than a simple bubbly attitude.

The girl takes three steps over and thrusts her arm out, palm extended, for a handshake. "I'm Blaire. It's goodtameetcha." All one word. Just like that. "I'd say I'm overjoyed but as you can tell from looking at me, I'm

SPELLING DISASTER

pretty much turned up to eleven all the time. You'll get used to it. If not, then you'll have to find other living arrangements, I'm afraid. I am what I am and who I am."

I shake her hand, her grip firm. Blaire might be super scary to behold, a vision in pink, but something about her has me feeling like I might have made my first friend in this place.

"I can appreciate that. I'm Yasmine. It's nice to meet you, too," I say.

This vision in pink, this boy-band lover and pop princess…she should overwhelm me.

For some reason, it's easier to look at her than it was with Amy, and my smile is genuine for the first time today.

"I'm sure, since you probably registered with Gladys, you were given the spiel about how you're going to like it here." Blaire drops onto her own bed with a small grunt, her skirt fluffing out around her like tiered icing on a cupcake. "I won't lie to you. It's a typical campus in some ways and not in others. You've probably already had your welcome to the misfit house."

I lift Gus to my cheek to nuzzle him. "Oh, yes. In the form of a dude walking out of the bathroom in nothing but a towel."

Blaire rolls her eyes. "You're lucky most of them wear towels instead of using their air magic to dry. Anyway, I promise I'll give you a real tour of this place tomorrow. Help you get settled in. Let me guess." Her lips purse. "Amy told you that you'll settle in just fine and pointed out the sights like a tour guide at Disney World? This is all wonder and magic and blah blah."

I cock my head at the term, knowing literally nothing about Disney World except that people love it. "She showed me to the dorm, yeah, and pointed out some sights on the way," I reply.

"As much as you look at me and think *extrovert*, this place is not the cozy ride Amy likes to make it out to be. She schmoozes the prospective students and is even worse with the recently accepted." Blaire points to her chest. "Stick with me, Yazzy. You'll be all right."

Funny thing is, I actually believe her, and the belief is strong enough to push aside my earlier reservations. If all the outcasts are like Blaire…then maybe I won't mind being one as well.

CHAPTER
EIGHT

I sleep like shit and my alarm takes me out of a nightmare where I'm racing through the library, on fire, and no one hears me screeching for help. Gee, I wonder where that one came from?

Except when I open my eyes, it isn't flames I see but bright sunlight shifting through cotton-candy pink blinds and a blurry Blaire on the other side of the room with headphones over her ears.

She's already dressed and ready, leaning back in the chair in front of her desk and bobbing her foot along to whatever music she's listening to. Probably one of the bands on the thousands of posters in our room.

How easy will it be to tug my sheets over my head and go back to sleep? Not that I really feel like sleeping after those night terrors, sweat still beading along my skin and making my clothes stick to me.

Blaire flicks her gaze at me when I force myself out of bed and lifts an eyebrow in my direction. "Better get ready," she says.

I nod and grab my shower caddy from my dresser, all purchased by the coven. Gus snoozes on my pillow right next to the indentation where my head had been.

The first day of classes are always stressful. I've heard enough stories from people detailing theirs, including Remi, who always wants to impress on me how horrible school is for her.

I thought maybe experiencing it myself would be different.

Why?

Ridiculously misplaced optimism.

I'm coming in blind and I'm coming in after the semester has already started, so my first day of class is nothing but one mistake after another. My schedule was indeed in the folder Gladys handed out, and although I make it to my first class in time, there's only one seat left in the back of the room underneath a perpetually drafty window.

In my next class, I sit in the wrong seat, apparently, only to be called out by several students who already claimed the space for their friends.

I trip over the flat floor in one of the classrooms, prompting enough laughter from my peers to curdle my stomach. The skirt is already a little tight around the hip area and the shirt too loose where my breasts should be. One look in the mirror this morning showed me my pale cheeks and dark circles under my eyes.

Everyone watches me take a seat and miss the actual seat by about three inches, dropping right onto my ass with my legs open and flashing my underpants for the world to see.

SPELLING DISASTER

Clumsy.

Embarrassed and clumsy, and now red-faced.

Especially when I'm busy jumping at shadows. Any small movement out of the corner of my eye has me remembering fog through a forest. Which is absolutely crazy because the Horned God and his magic hasn't followed me here.

I'm late for my third and fourth classes of the day. Not because I got lost but because for some reason, the clock moves much faster than my feet carry me.

I can't catch a break. It's as if someone has hexed me.

Halfway through the food line at lunch, I miscalculate the distance between my tray and my chest and end up with minestrone soup down my front.

The lady at the end of the line, swiping my dining card, clicks her tongue. "Honey, you're still paying for it even if you're wearing it," she warns me.

My cheeks flame, and I hustle with the rest of my tray toward an empty table in the corner of the room. In the shadows and alone. Where I belong.

I have to watch each step I take to make sure I don't trip again because suddenly I've lost control of my feet and my legs.

"Yo, Yazzy! You are not sitting by yourself." Blaire motions for me to join her at her table. She's surrounded by a couple people who eye me strangely but don't say a word against me joining them. "Even though you're super embarrassing right now. Do you have enough time to head back to the room to change?"

Probably not, given how my day is going.

I plop down across from her with a groan. "No, I

don't, and things are not going my way right now. Today seems to be particularly stressful," I tell her.

Her smile is sympathetic as she pretends not to notice the way her friends move away from me, just a little bit. "Girl, it's going to be fine. You're probably harsher on yourself than you have to be. You'll find your footing."

"Not before my face meets the floor a few more times." I can't even blame this on my nerves. I've always done really well in an academic setting. Sure, this is new to me, but I've been homeschooled. I've been trained my whole life to ascend.

So what's wrong with me?

I stare morosely at Blaire until a flash of color over her shoulder catches my eye. And I sit up straighter, my focus laser-like and immediately captured.

Wow.

The guy stands a head taller than his companions with a swath of wavy auburn hair hanging over his face. Broad shoulders, a wicked smile, and dark eyes. The smile isn't for me, not anywhere close, but I want it to be.

My mouth goes dry the longer I stare at him. Handsome, mischievous, and apparently popular, if the large group of people clustering around him is an indication.

"Who is that?" I ask Blaire.

I've never seen anyone who looks like him before. Not even the heroes of my romance novels.

Blaire twists around in her seat and her expression sours when she sees the object of my attention. "Oh, that's Theo Acaster. Girls tend to throw themselves at him like he's Mr. Hotshot. He's tall, good looking, charming…" she trails off.

"You say those things like they're bad." I watch him from the far side of the dining room. Theo swaggers up to a table of friends and is greeted with rousing applause from our classmates.

"Honey, no." Blaire turns back to me and snaps her fingers until she's sure she has my attention. "I can see you're interested, probably want to start sniffing around his heels, and just no. Stop right now before you get your sights set on him. He's not for people like us."

I blink until she comes into focus even though I'm still completely aware of Theo. Standing, sitting, talking, grinning. Breathing, even. "Why?" I ask.

"Because he is totally out of your league. I'm not saying it to be a bitch or because I want him for myself," Blaire warns. Her lips thin, her gaze searching mine. No, she's not trying to be mean, but her words hurt regardless. "It's just true. Dudes like him don't go for girls like you, who live in X House. The path he's going, he's going to end up as a high priest somewhere high profile." She stares me down, meaning business. "And it won't be with a misfit on his arm."

"It's not like I'm ready to get married or anything serious." I'm all flustered.

"Better to stop you before you let those stars in your eyes carry you away."

I've already been lumped into the *do not touch* category because of my housing arrangements. It isn't fair and a part of me wants to buck against Blaire's words because I'm much more than where I sleep.

Another part of me, the latest part, knows she's right.

When you're a Golden Boy like Theo appears to be, then you have to stay in your lane and even if I didn't live in X House, I'd be beneath him. Or at least in a completely different league. The homeschooled nerd who has no friends versus the alpha-male popular guy?

Yeah, it's not a match that happens in real life.

Still, there's something about him drawing me forward and I have to admit, I'm curious. Even when I watch a girl walk out from the crowd and put her arms around Theo's waist. She latches onto him, her chest to his back, and his arms twine over hers as his smile tenses. He pats her hand with his but makes no move to cuddle her close or return her affection.

I sit up a little straighter.

"Ah, there she is," Blaire continues with a groan. "Where one goes, there's the other. That's Helena. The Barbie to his Ken."

"The what?" I ask.

She turns to me and flicks her hair over her shoulder. "You know. Barbie and Ken. Because they're the perfect couple, blah blah. Totally plastic. Those two are on and off so many times it's hard to keep track of whether they're official or not."

I have no idea what she's talking about, the reference flying over my head, and I've never been so aware of my sheltered past as I am right now.

"Come on. You know," Blaire continues, urging me

to get it. "Barbie. Ken. Plastic pink shoes and fun house and…okay, you have no idea what I'm saying, do you?"

"Are you going to judge me if I say no?"

Blaire shakes her head. "Not judge, exactly. But I'm curious. Why are you here now and why are you so late? Did someone find you in the woods being raised by a pack of wolves or something?"

"No, nothing like that," I reply with a small, tight laugh.

"So, what's your deal, Yazzy?"

In my gut I wonder if Blaire will accept any fiction, like Amy and the others did. Probably not. She looks like a bubblegum princess but she's quick-witted and sharp.

"It's just a late start. Things kind of got away from me," I hedge. Not willing to let anyone know the truth about me.

The less she knows, the better. I'm not willing to compromise. Until she presses, I'll need to keep it surface level.

Blaire stares at me, waiting for an answer, and when I simply grimace at her, she deflates. "Fine, don't tell me anything," she says with a sniff. "I'm just your roommate and the only friend you've got here, but whatever." Suddenly her eyes brighten and she reaches out to slap my hand away from the fork I'd just driven into my salad. "The food here sucks. As you can see because you're wearing it, the quality is about as bare minimum as they can get. Go on, grab your stuff."

"Why would I grab my stuff?" I try to lift my fork and once again get my fingers slapped.

"Because I've got an idea. I'm taking you off campus." Blaire sinks her teeth into her idea and refuses to back down. "There's a whole world out there and, call it my intuition, but I think it's high time you see some of it. Plus, a good meal will help you."

No one said anything about being allowed off campus but it doesn't seem like the kind of thing students are encouraged to do. Considering the fence around the entire academy property, the giant gate, all of it.

I really don't want to continue my day of absolute bad luck with getting in trouble for leaving right after I arrive.

But...

Blaire is the first friend I've had, maybe in my entire life, and she seems interested in me. She didn't come to me through my much more popular sister, either, as most of my acquaintances have until this point.

Blaire is sticking up for me for me and not out of a sense of duty.

I push my tray away and reach down for my shoulder bag. "Sure. Let's go," I tell her.

"Excellent!" She crows out and her voice echoes through the entire room.

Not that any conversation stops.

Not that Theo and Helena stop snuggling like lovers across the room.

I drop my eyes to my feet and follow Blaire out and away from the public display of affection making me itchy in the wrong way. There's no way I'm jealous over a stranger...I tell myself.

"Let's stop and grab a different shirt for you. Then, we're outta here!" Blaire flings her arms out on either side of her head.

"Where do you want to go?" I ask.

"I've got the perfect place. Trust me. And it's only about a five-minute walk so we can be there and back in no time." She picks up the pace until we're back at the dorm so I can change.

Do I trust her? Not particularly, when she forces me to grab one of her vibrant pink shirts and shove it over my head, or when she herds me out through a hole in the fence.

Especially not when we stand in front of a massive building with a blue-and-white sign that looks like it's about three acres of space.

"Welcome!" Blaire exclaims. "To the best big box store in town. Well, the only big box store in town. You're going to love it."

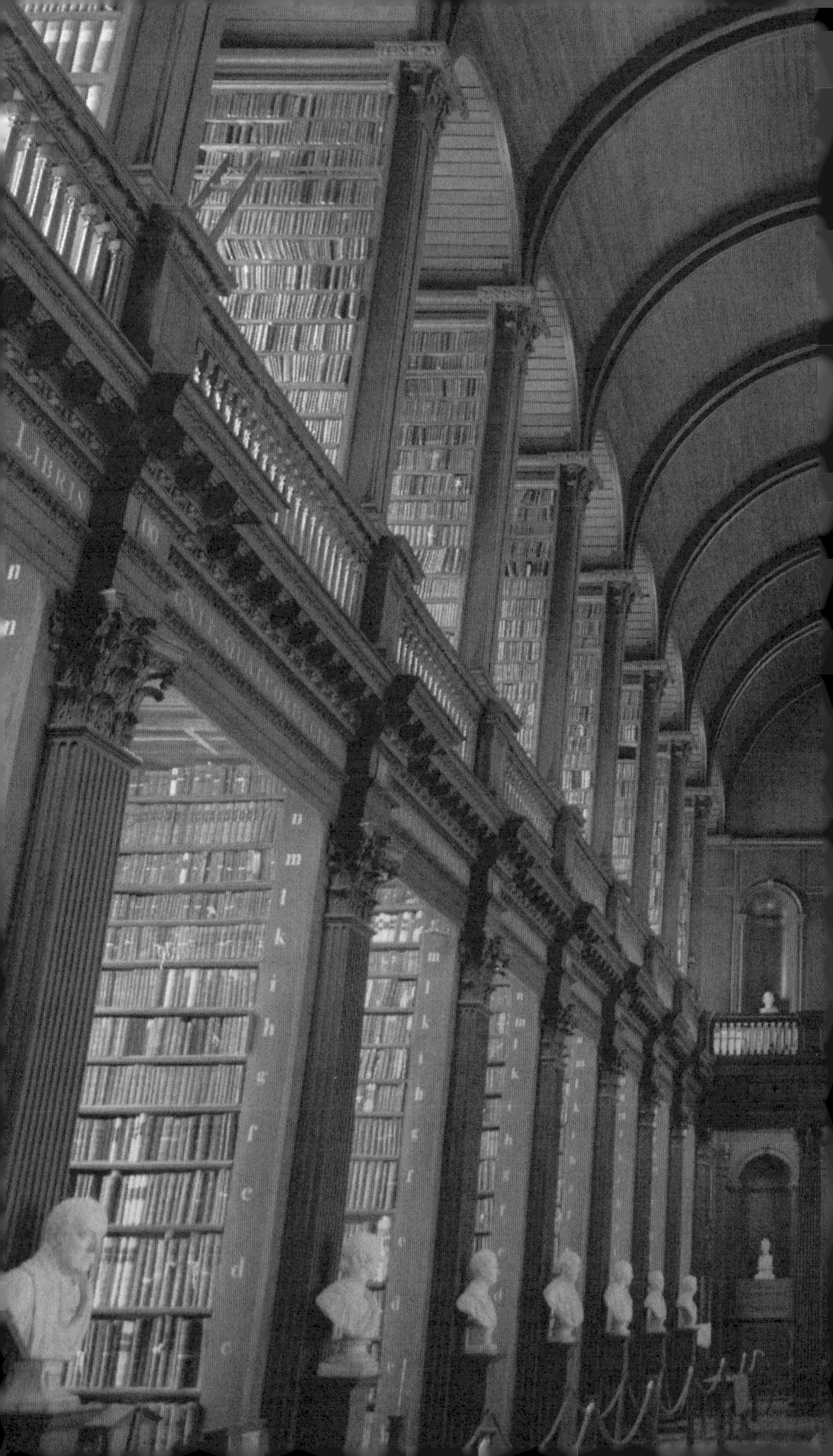

CHAPTER NINE

Having never been to one of these "box stores" in my life, I have no damn clue what to expect. I take a minute to study the strange territory, mustering up my usual curiosity.

This isn't a book, and although there might be a time limit, I'm finally getting a chance to explore someplace outside of my comfort zone and have an adventure.

Blaire must sense my nerves, too, because she reaches behind her to link our hands together and gives me a tug. "Follow my lead and it's going to be fine!" She studies me. "You really have no clue about this. It's cute, in a way. You're adorable."

"I don't feel adorable," I say as she sails through the sliding front doors and into the fluorescent lit wilderness of this concrete monstrosity. "I feel out of control."

"There's nothing wrong with being out of control."

"Apparently there is, if it means I get a little spooked in places like this." It's wonderful and terrifying at the same time, so many people inside and more things to buy than seems decent.

Blaire barks out a laugh and replies with, "Any normal person with half a brain would get spooked by this. It's madness on the best days."

I squeeze her hand, grateful for something to hold on to, only to have her break away seconds later.

"You know, before I enrolled at the academy, I lived in the human world," she says, grabbing a cart. "Went to places like this all the time."

She flings her purse into the smaller part in the front and I do the same with my bag. Then, maneuvering through the rows of food, she takes off and leaves me no choice but to jog to catch up to her.

Mouth closed, I tell myself.

No need to look as awed as I am or to let anyone know this is abnormal to me.

"Straddling both worlds isn't the easiest, mind you, but I made it work and did it with a lot of flair."

"I bet you did," I giggle.

"I even went to school there," she's saying grandly. "It was a trade school where I studied cosmetology. It was amazing! I loved listening to the women and helping them with their problems. I'm sure you've already guessed this about me, but I actually have a knack for makeovers. So much so that it caught the attention of the school."

"Andora?" I clarified.

"Yeah. Apparently I'm a natural at transformation magic. Which isn't really a thing anymore, not without a whole lot of preparation and ingredients, which is why they put me in X House."

A natural at transformation magic… yes, it fits. Blaire has the air of someone who is absolutely skilled at owning their looks, their aesthetic, and changing it on a whim. I fight against the urge to tug on a lock of my very plain black hair. The same color it's always been.

I've never even dyed it. I've never worn makeup or had my bushy eyebrows plucked or primped. What had Remi called my style?

She said it fit not only my clothes but my face, too.

And not for lack of desire, either. There have been plenty of times in the past I stared at myself in the mirror and wondered how I'd look with green hair. With bangs. With a fringe, or something wild and crazy, like rainbow ombre. How about eyeshadow or lipstick?

What would Blaire do if she got her hands on me? Maybe one day, if we stay close, I'll ask her to work her magic on me.

"How did it feel?" I ask her. "To live and work in the human world? Was it weird?"

She turns to smile over her shoulder at me. "It was pretty cool, I admit. Even when I felt a little like an outsider because of what I am, seeing those women leave happy after sitting with me, I made a difference. You know? But once the school reached out to me, they offered a scholarship to come and learn and hone my craft and I had to accept. It seemed like one of those opportunities you'd be pretty stupid to pass up."

"For sure. You've got to go for it," I agree. "It's an opportunity."

"An adventure," she corrects, echoing my earlier thought, "and I'm all for adventure. And I agreed to accept the scholarship as long as I could continue with my signature style and not be tied down by the dress code rules." Blaire stops pushing the cart, holding her arms out at her side and turning in a slow circle for me. "We had to compromise. It took me a few weeks to convince the board who runs the place to let me do what I do."

I wonder why the academy decided to work with Blaire rather than enforcing their rules.

Although I have to admit, she's convincing; she got me out of my shell.

Until she continues with, "I'm the only witch there who has transformation magic naturally." She blushes a pretty pink rose color. It matches her hair. "I don't say it because I have a big head or anything. Apparently, it's true. I'm being groomed, as it is, to do great things for the magic world," she finishes. "Or so the headmaster told me."

"I don't think you have a big head," I tell her with a smile. "Well, any bigger than normal. I think it's amazing. If you've got the skill then of course you want to use it for the magic world."

The store is massive and crazy and fun. There's so much to see I can't stop from swinging my head from one side of the aisle to the other.

Blaire realizes, after a while, and stops to chuckle at my wonder.

"Your eyes are all wide, Yazzy. And your mouth has that kinda gaping thing going on at all the options," she says. "There you go being adorable again."

"This place is awesome."

"I think, in order to work magic well, you're going to need to know about the mortal realm. It's the world and the people you're protecting from the magic around you, the power you wield," Blaire continues.

A little too somber for my peace of mind.

"I don't think I'm ready for a lesson like that," I admit.

"Okay, that's fine." Blaire's face splits in a wild grin. "Let's shop, then. Grab some snacks for later once you realize the dining hall serves glop."

It isn't a good idea for me to miss my only afternoon class, not on my first day. Which I tell Blaire, hoping she'll understand the time limit, and she tells me that it's not going to be a big deal. What *is* a big deal is soaking in the atmosphere. And after a few more minutes of exploring, she breaks down my defenses and I agree.

Instead of worrying, I have fun in the toy aisle. I grab a bag of chips, and explore a freezer section that makes me ready for winter.

When was the last time I let myself just let go and enjoy? To spend an afternoon laughing without any kind of stress?

I can't remember.

There's always been something to do, some kind of pressing responsibility that needs my immediate attention. Or Mom there reminding me of what waited for me in my future.

This time, it's for me. And although it's really difficult to let go, I try; being around Blaire helps. She doesn't judge me for being confused by certain things about the mortal realm. In fact, she's got the patience of a saint with me.

We make it back to campus a little later than we should and just in time for curfew. Blaire wipes imaginary sweat from her brow the moment we're on the front stoop of X House.

"See? I told you it was all going to work out." Blaire spins in a wide circle with bags in each hand acting as counterbalance. "We had a great time, and we didn't get in trouble. Not to mention we've got some great things."

I laugh, silently thanking whatever good luck put me in the misfit house with Blaire as my roommate. We're opposites in a lot of ways, but it's a good thing. If anyone is going to get me to be more confident, then it's her, without a shadow of a doubt.

"Say it," she prompts as she drops her arms back to her sides. "Say I was right, Yazzy. I need to hear you say it out loud."

"You were right," I reply with a chuckle. Until my breath catches in my chest again because there's Theo.

God, he really is gorgeous. Each step radiates assurance, the kind that doesn't come from being forced but is naturally nurtured until it's simply the way you operate.

The strands of auburn hair catch the light of the moon overhead and gild his features in glowing silver.

I gulp hard enough for Blaire to hear.

He doesn't seem to be racing back across campus

quickly. Not the same way Blaire and I had to hustle to get back to X House.

"Why isn't he hurrying?" I want to know.

Blaire scoffs. "Because the boys don't have to adhere to the same rigid routines and curfews like the girls. I mean, they have curfew, but the rules bend more for them. And partially because he's Theo. Okay, partially because his family's money is what helps keep the school afloat."

Ah, so he comes from money. I should have guessed. Money paves the way for so many things in this world, whether mortal or witch.

"You find that attractive about him?" Blaire presses with sweetness I know is false.

I elbow Blaire. "God, no. Just him, whether he's poor or otherwise. But you're a wealth of information. And advice."

"Of course I am! You stick with me, and I'll never lead you astray." She casts me a sideways grin. "I've got your back. Even if the truth sucks, I'll be real with you. It's the best thing one friend can do for another."

"It's been a long time since I felt like anyone—" I break off.

I don't know why, but guilt stirs for feeling like Blaire is one of the only people who has seen me for me and not what I can bring to the table.

In any kind of relationship, friendly or otherwise.

"Hey, it's fine," Blaire says. "You don't have to get all mushy with me right now. We're roomies. We've got time to get to know each other better."

"Plus, I'm beat," I add.

We make it back to the room just in time. Gus jumps up from the small bed he's made on my desk and twitches his whiskers in greeting.

Took you long enough.

I grin. "It's good to see you too, little buddy. Hopefully you found ways to keep yourself occupied today."

What occupied me was being stuck in this house. Don't worry, I've memorized the escape routes just in case.

"Oh, yeah. By the way—" Blaire rushes to close the door behind us. "You shouldn't let anyone see him or you'll get into trouble. This place...likes magic they can contain. Predictable magic."

My spine straightens. "You think they'll make me get rid of him?"

No. Hell no. There's no chance I'm sending Gus away.

"Familiars are not predictable magic," Blaire explains. "Just be really careful that no one sees him anywhere or else it's not going to end well. There are definitely some rules you have to adhere to. The clothing? It's harmless. Familiars? They don't always play within the rules."

"Noted."

I'll have to keep Gus hidden. Because he's not going anywhere.

CHAPTER TEN

It takes me a few weeks to get used to the adjustment of living on campus. The rules help, the schedule helps. Those are things I'm used to. Waking up at a certain time, knowing what to expect out of my day, it all helps. There's a different sort of continuity to this place, one I can appreciate.

Even with Blaire grumbling about how the rigidity makes her uncomfortable.

And because my mother made sure to pass all those things along to me to prepare me, I'm actually decently ahead in my classes. Not just caught up, the way I'd hoped. Ahead.

My initial week of feeling hexed and clumsy gives way to feeling more at ease when I raise my hand and call out the right answer.

Or whenever we're paired up to execute a spell and my skill shines through.

Even getting tested for my powers and still being placed in X House can't dim my slow budding joy.

The professors say I'm quite advanced in my studies and astute in witchy ways.

The first time I heard one of them say it, I squirmed in my seat fighting off a smile. I always thought to myself that I'd be behind if I had to go to a regular class. It's a nice surprise to be told the opposite.

Studying comes easily to me, too.

At least, it does unless I'm around Theo.

We have a few classes together and the first time I saw him sit a few rows ahead of me, I turned to mush. Every brain cell did a little happy dance before checking out for the day.

With him, I turn into a blubbering mess, and I have trouble remembering my own name. I stare at his back until I've memorized the planes of muscle beneath the fabric of his shirt.

No, not like some stalker.

Maybe a little.

I'm not going out of my way to learn everything there is to know about him. I'm just curious. And I like to look.

Just as Blaire said, Theo is definitely the *hot guy* on campus. Quintessential hot guy. All the girls fawn over him despite him having a girlfriend, or so it appears to me. Helena is always around and although I haven't gotten a whiff of whether they're on or off, it seems to me they're on.

I've read enough romance novels to understand one key facet about this situation: Theo doesn't even know I exist.

SPELLING DISASTER

Which is made painfully clear the next day in class during group participation.

"Class," the professor begins. "Can anyone tell me the most crucial element for turning common stones into gold?"

I lift my hand. "The philosopher's stone?" If it worked for Harry Potter in the books, then maybe it will work for me. It's my pathetic attempt to add a little humor.

A few snickers answer me.

"Sorry, Miss Williams, that's incorrect." The professors smiles tightly at me before pointing toward another student with their hand raised. "Yes, go ahead."

Okay, so this isn't a place for jokes. My knowledge and skills are all I have, besides Blaire, and it's not fair for her to have to babysit me all the time. Theo doesn't turn in his seat to stare at me like some of his friends do, most of them with derision and only a little bit of pity.

I've learned to live with both.

I raise my hand a few more times, the only one who does, offering up several more correct answers to the questions asked. The snide remarks from the others keep coming.

"*Homeschool* is trying to become the teacher's pet," someone whispers.

"Look at her trying. Like acting so pathetic will get her attention or something."

My face burns, trying to ignore the remarks.

"I'd like to point out that Yasmine is not the only one who can raise her hand," the teacher offers. "All of you are more than welcome to give me answers when I ask for them."

The classroom falls into dead silence.

Focus on that, I tell myself. Focus on the applause and reward for my skills when I'm not cracking jokes.

The applause and reward for my skill are a benefit. Not something to be embarrassed about.

Despite the havoc that comes in the wake of it all.

The professor claps her hands. "Now, today we're going to be making a poultice in class. Who wants to tell me what sunflowers can be used for in this instance?"

I slide my hand underneath my thigh to keep from lifting it. Another girl to the left of me shoots her hand up to be called on.

"Sunflowers are used for clairvoyance," she answers.

We're talking about poultices, so why is the girl...no, she's not joking. She's just wrong.

"Sorry, Professor?" I've got my hand lifted in the air once again. "Sunflowers are not used for clairvoyance, but to detoxify."

"Yes, that's correct, Yasmine."

An audible groan sounds from behind me and I shrink down into myself instinctively.

"Christ, someone can't learn how to keep her mouth shut, can she?" The girl at the desk to the right of me, one of Helena's minions, flips her hair over her shoulder and the temperature in the room changes visibly.

My breath puffs out in a white cloud in front of my face.

"That's enough, Kimberly." The professor waves her hands in front of her and the charge in the air dissipates. "I won't have you poking fun at someone in my classroom, especially when your own grades are slipping towards southern territories."

Someone lets out a strangled laugh until Kimberly whirls to glare at them, her expression causing the sound to cut off.

"I don't understand what I'm doing wrong," I tell Blaire once I'm back in the room. When it's just the two of us, I relax. "If I know the answer, then why shouldn't I say it? Especially if someone else gets it wrong. They could hurt themselves or someone else if they're not corrected. It's for safety more than anything else."

Blaire rolls her eyes when I refuse to sit down. "Because no one corrects Courtney Biggins. Don't you get it, girl? She's like witch royalty."

"Courtney Biggins?" I repeat.

"Yeah, the one with the large gold hoop earrings. It doesn't matter if she says the wrong thing. She's the kind of person you do not correct. Like, *ever*. All you need to do is nod and smile and wave when she wants you to."

It sounds exhausting.

Trying to keep up with the unspoken rules of this place will run me right into the ground and, even with Blaire's constant corrections, I'm lagging seriously behind.

My head gives a twitch of pain.

"How would I know these things without you?" I sound as pathetic as I feel.

"You don't," she replies. "You have me as your guide and your guru. You're going to have to accept it. Hell, even if you went to a normal high school, this would still be an adjustment." She spins around in her chair with her headphones draped over her neck and her eyes painted to match her socks.

Pink, of course.

"Do you think I made a bad impression?" I ask, biting my thumbnail.

"Oh, definitely." Her agreement without hesitation has the blood now draining from my face and pooling somewhere on the floor between my feet.

"I didn't know."

"Of course you didn't. Let's hope you didn't do enough damage to permanently impact your reputation," Blaire insists.

I groan. "What reputation? I'm the weirdest kid in the misfit house. All facts in my head and no social skills." I tap the side of my head. "There's something seriously wrong with me."

Which I find out soon enough. With Courtney's disapproval, I'm quickly shut out of everything. The few people who sat at my table at lunch have moved on to other seats. There are no study buddies for classes where I want a little extra help or attention.

Not even the other misfits in the house will spend more than half a second of their time acknowledging me. Only Blaire, and probably only because she's my roommate so there is no escape. Apparently, if this place is a prison, then Courtney is the warden.

Or some kind of gatekeeper.

And at first, I'm optimistic the freeze-out won't last. Until another week goes by and things shift from bad to worse.

The alarm clangs shrilly from the nightstand next to my face and knocks me out of a dream about the library. A good one this time, thankfully. There're no flames, only familiar stacks, and Remi waiting for me around a corner. Smiling. Offering me a hand.

I like to think it's out of this mess I've made for myself.

Except the second my brain switches on from sleep to reality, I know the dream is only wishful thinking. My subconscious showing me something comforting where I've felt in control in the past.

There's no control here. Even when I think I'm doing something right, like calling out the answers in class, it's wrong. Alienating.

Stretching, I run my fingers through my hair and come up short on the right side.

Long layers on the left, down to my breasts, curling slightly.

Nothing past my shoulder on the right.

A gasp rips from my throat and I sit straight up in bed, gritting my teeth and blindly tugging on the short strands of hair.

Gus squeaks, jostled awake when he drops from my chest to my lap. *What happened? Are you okay?*

No, not okay. Something is wrong. My chest tightens

and it's a struggle to grab him and gently, slowly, place him aside before I head toward the mirror on top of Blaire's dresser.

The gasp turns into a groan at my reflection and the partially cut hair.

"Oh my god." It looks like someone took gardening shears and lopped off everything on the right half of my head. I stare at myself with my eyes wide and my face blanches. "What happened?" Tears prick the back of my eyes.

Blaire's shower caddy is gone. A quick glance at the clock shows she's right on schedule, the schedule that she hates.

Gus hops up on to the dresser with a squeak. *It's a hex. A magical hex. Someone must have cast a spell on you at some point yesterday.*

I gawk at him. "Are you kidding?"

This sort of thing happens when someone in your immediate vicinity works one to place on you. In one of your classes, maybe?

"Gus, what can I do?" Tears leak out and burn paths down my cheeks. "There's no way I can go to class like this. How are we going to fix this mess?" I run my fingers through the strands hoping to be able to gather it into a ponytail, but the mess at the back of my head still looks bad.

Don't freak out, Gus tries to say.

Are you kidding me right now? I answer back. *It's impossible to keep my control.* Not like I'm so attached to my hair I'm going to melt down, but someone hexed me. Which means someone hates me enough to do something horrible rather than talk to me.

You don't have to go to class with your hair cut off. Or hexed in any way. We just need a protection spell. Something that will counteract the hex and keep you protected the next time someone tries to sling magic your way.

A protection spell.

It's a struggle to get my breathing under control again, to order my thoughts enough to consider the next step in front of me. Too easy to lose myself to the thought that one of my peers dislikes me enough to hex me.

What if the hex hadn't stopped at my hair? What if it had taken something else from me, or done any real damage?

"I've read about those kinds of spells," I comment out loud to Gus. "Only in books, though. I've never tried to do it on my own before."

It's not hard. Gus's whiskers flick. *I can walk you through it. Except you're going to have to find other ways to keep the bullies at bay. The protection spell won't last for long. It's all on you to try and—*

If you tell me I need to be nice and make friends then I really will freak out, I warn him.

I wasn't going to tell you to make friends. I was going to tell you to watch your back. You've got to find a way to deal with these people.

"Will the spell get rid of the hex? Fix my hair?" I ask.

It should, yes.

I draw a breath into my aching chest and wait for

the sense of relief to come. I have a plan and a course of action except, for some reason, the relief never comes.

"Okay." I prepare for the worst and face Gus, force a smile. "Show me what I need to do."

He's right; once we get started, it's not hard to complete the sequence of events. I remember bits and pieces of things I've read about protection spells in the past and put them all together like following a recipe.

Gus knows the correct words to root the spell; all we need to do is gather the ingredients. Most of them are readily available on the school grounds or in the apothecary kits every student is required to have.

Luckily for me, I've got what we need right here on my desk.

Keep the bullies at bay, though…I have no idea how long the protection spell is going to last or what it's going to work against. Hexes, sure, but what else? What other things are the bullies planning for me?

Gus and I make it through the protection spell, and I don't feel any different afterward.

"Why isn't my hair growing back?" I ask.

The hex is no longer viable, but the damage is already done, it seems. I'm sorry.

My lower lip trembles and, ashamed, I bite down on it hard. "It's not your fault, Gus. Thank you for helping me."

The protection spell is one step toward making this right, sure. What next? Worry eats away at my insides. Things are going to get worse from here or so I'm afraid.

"Oh, honey. Your hair!"

I glance up at the sound of Blaire's voice as she pushes through the door, fresh from her shower. She waves a hand in front of her face to clear the residual smoke from the burning sage out of her way. "What did you do?"

"That's implying I'm the one who did this," I say. Pushing aside the sadness, frustration, and worry for the future. "I woke up this way."

"I know it wasn't you. You would have come to me before doing anything drastic, so still the viper tongue and let me take a look at this."

She sets her shower caddy down by her dresser, still wrapped in a fluffy towel the color of cotton candy. It's knotted at the front and holds in place as she bends down in front of me and touches the frayed edges of my hair.

"Apparently it's some kind of hex," I say. "I have no idea where it came from."

I stay still while she runs her finger through the strands of hair around my face, fluffing and examining those rough chopped edges.

"I guess it doesn't matter where it came from. What matters is fixing it." Blaire draws in a breath. "Good work with the protection spell but it's not going to help you regrow your hair. No matter what anyone tells you." She narrows her eyes at Gus almost as though she knows what he said to me.

"I had high hopes. It was my first time trying one."

She grins at me. "Bang up job, then. Let's see what we can do about the hair. Leave it to me. This is a time when my transformation magic is going to come in handy. Not to mention that I've been hoping you'd let me get my claws into you for some time."

Blaire directs me on where to sit.

I don't move. "I...I appreciate you looking for a silver lining, but..." My voice trails off as pending tears sting my eyes. "But I don't think I can. Not right now."

I like to think there is something out there helping to right the wrongs of the universe, but I'm having a hard time being optimistic these days.

My world, everything I knew and loved, came to a screeching halt and I found myself here. Andora Academy might be a great place. It might be a wonderful spot to learn, with opportunities to grow my powers and become a powerful witch in my own right.

I'm naive.

I'm hopeless.

Because I thought I'd be able to do what I've always done when that isn't the case at all.

I go to class with my new fringe hairdo. No one says anything about the change except for a few under-the-breath whispers I can't make out.

That night, once the lights are out and curfew in place, I bite back more tears and wish for home.

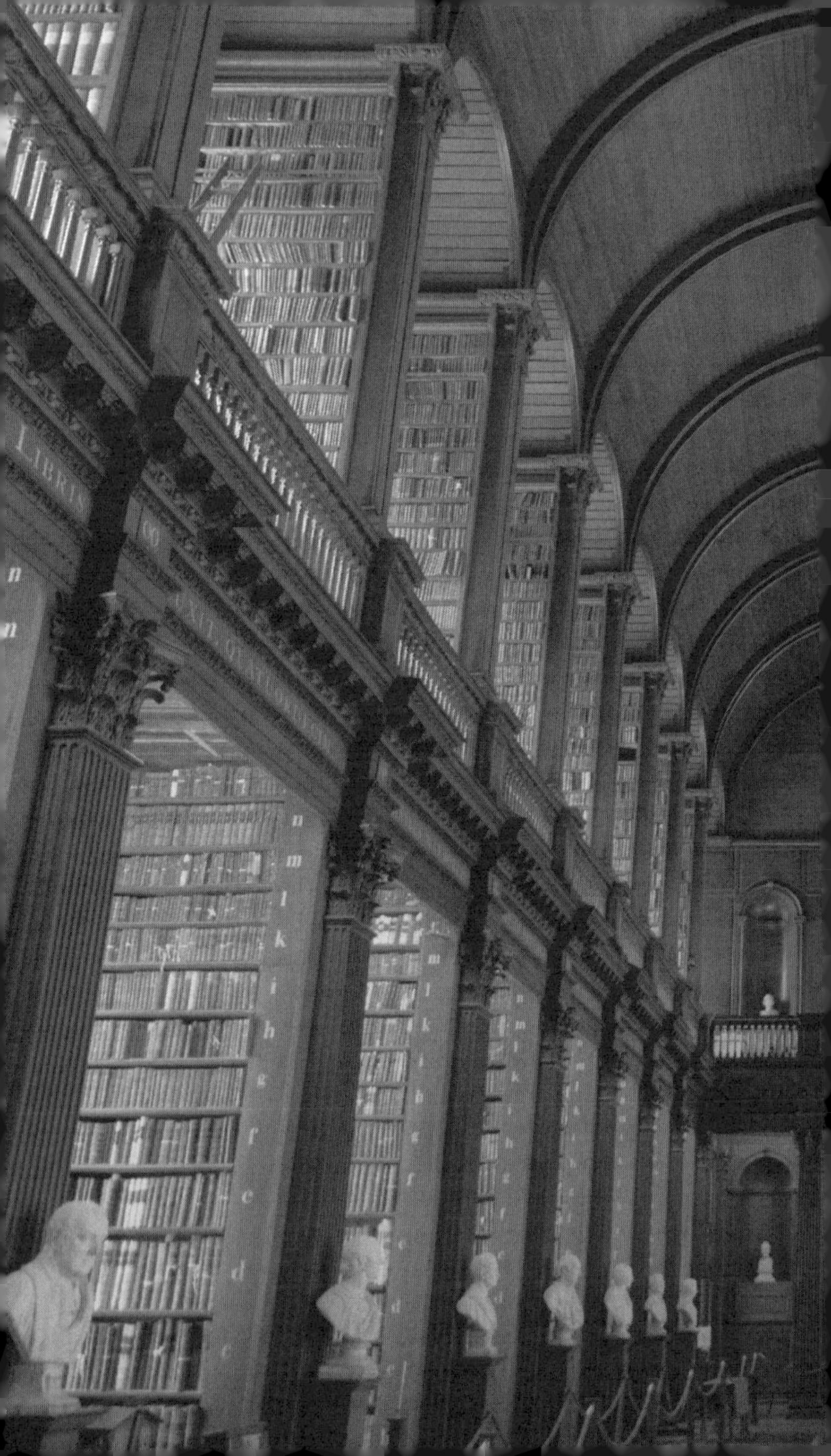

CHAPTER
ELEVEN

In a strange turn of events that feels like a distinctive slap in the face rather than anything synchronous, we're practicing how to change metal to gold in alchemy class the following day.

The universe has a sick sense of humor sometimes and now it seems my joke from the other day has made it into the classroom.

I cast a glance at the ceiling and its worn beams, silently beseeching the powers that be to go easy on me. Not that I plan to make any more jokes about it but still.

There are no more whispers about my hair because, as Blaire assures me, it's yesterday's news.

I am yesterday's news.

I keep my eyes open and my ears trained for any more snide remarks or hastily whispered insults. When I hear nothing, see nothing, I still can't relax. Hypervigilance has turned me paranoid.

I'm constantly staring over my shoulder waiting for

something else to happen but there are no more whispered words and no more hexes.

The protection spell must be doing its job.

I send a mental high five down the connection to Gus to let him know, without words, it worked.

Either the protection is holding or the popular click really has decided I'm not worth their time anymore. I mentally cross my fingers for the latter. I've been working toward something bigger than me my whole life, I reason. It's past time for me to worry about what others think of me.

Saying it in my head doesn't help, though. It's a mantra I pay no attention to.

"Everything you need for today's alchemical reaction is in your booklet and the ingredients are on your desktop," the professor calls out. "I'm not going to set a time limit with today's exercise but of course, you only have until the end of class to complete the assignment. I'd like you all to give this your best shot. Not that you will be keeping the gold, mind you. I'll be turning it all back to metal by the end of the day."

"How much do you want to bet he's slipping some in his pocket?" someone hisses out.

A couple of chuckles follow.

I've already read and reread the instructions for today until I feel like I've got a good handle on what to do.

Grabbing a bowl of sage and purposely keeping my attention away from Theo, away from wondering if he noticed my haircut, I get to work. Blaire isn't in alchemy with me and, unsurprisingly, no one wants to work at my desktop as a pair. Which is okay. I'm better off doing it on my own.

I've got the ingredients laid out like a chef's workspace with everything in its place ready to go.

The professor stands at the front of the classroom ready to answer any questions. "You've got it well in hand," he continues as if we're in need of encouragement. "Keep it steady, try not to get too caught up in logistics."

And right off the bat, the person sharing the desk with Theo raises his hand.

"Can you come help?" the guy asks. "We're having a bit of a hard time here."

Theo elbows his friend in the side to get him to shut up.

"I mean, I'm the one having a hard time. It's like I can't get the steps to match up," his friend corrects.

"What seems to be the problem over here, gentlemen?"

The professor shifts over to their table and taps down on the book with the directions.

Except, I notice, Theo's friend isn't the one having the issues, not really. As we proceed alchemizing the hunk of scrap metal in the wooden bowl in front of us, *Theo* is the one with questions. He hesitates, second guessing everything he does.

And while I have it easy, it seems Theo is having problems.

He's trying not to make it obvious, but his friend keeps calling the professor over for clarification. Until it gets to the point where they start working separately and soon the other guy has a pile of gold in front of him while the apple of my eye does not.

I stop what I'm doing—cleaning up as I've been done for fifteen minutes—to watch Theo do his best not to let the others see him struggle. Cocking my head to the side, I study him openly. Wondering how he expects to keep others from noticing, and how long he's been at it.

Long enough to fool me.

The rest of the class sees it, too, although they must prefer to stay quiet about it rather than point out the obvious. Theo needs help.

I keep part of my attention on him for the rest of the period. The metal in front of me has been alchemized and arranged into neat piles of gold brick long before the bell rings to signal the end of class.

The professor claps his hands and calls time.

"Class, wonderful job today. I'm proud of all of you, whether you managed to actually accomplish the task or not." He smiles around at the students who are scrambling to get their stuff and get out.

Everyone else hurries to escape, either to study hall or to their next class.

I stay behind and linger for nothing short of curiosity, still focused on Theo. Rather than cleaning up, he's staring at his pile of metal like he's expecting to get a miracle. Or answers. Neither of which happen.

"Mr. Acaster, if you don't mind, I'd like to have a word with you?" the professor asks.

Theo jolts at the sound of his name.

"Ah, sure, Professor. I'll stay."

I'm not supposed to listen. I know it's bad form to

listen. I can't force myself to move until there's only me and Theo left behind, and neither he nor the teacher are aware of me.

"Now, I'm sure this is not what you want to hear. I hate to be the one to say this, or to make you feel as though you've been called out in front of your friends," the professor begins.

"No, it's okay," Theo assures him, kind rather than rattled. "Go ahead."

"Quite frankly, your grades this semester are poor, to say the least." It's a whisper. Barely there, and yet every word rings louder than the clang of a hammer on an anvil. "If you do not open yourself up to some much-needed help then you are at serious risk of failing. I'd hate for your witchy dreams to go poof. Do you understand?"

Theo is silent for a long time. "I understand."

He's solemn, pale.

"Your family donates a lot of money to this school so the other professors may not feel comfortable talking to you about such matters. They may even be content to let you slide by under the radar and push you through when your attention flags. I am not one of them. Mr. Acaster, you have the makings of a fine spellcaster, tempered by your attitude and sensibility. None of those things will matter if you don't apply yourself."

"What do you suggest I do?" Theo wants to know.

"Personally, if I were in your shoes, then I'd find a tutor," the professor continues. "It would be in your best interest. Someone who grasps concepts easily and may be able to explain them to you on your level."

Theo stiffens before saying, "My level?" His jaw clenches.

"In a way you will understand better than the way I have been explaining things," the professor explains. "Technical jargon is getting in your way. I'm not sure how you plan to juggle studies, baseball, and tutoring, but you'll find a way. You'll figure it out."

"Fine," Theo grinds out.

I've stayed too long.

Trying not to let either of them know I heard, I shove my last book into my bag and hurry for the door. Shoot, eavesdropping was wrong and I know it. I'm a third of the way across the expansive campus green when the heavy thud of footfalls catches up to me, and at first I'm too lost to notice the sound.

Until a hand drops on my shoulder and sends me shooting out of my skin.

"Hold on. Yasmine? Wait a second. I want to talk to you. Hey, sorry, I didn't mean to scare you."

Theo catches up to me and the surprise of hearing my name come out of his mouth turns my legs into icicles once I come back to my body. Staring at him, just staring, up close and personal for the first time.

Be cool, be cool.

"You…oh, you didn't scare me." I sound the complete opposite of cool.

I had no idea he knew my name.

Every atom of my being is now attuned to his presence.

"I called your name, but I guess you didn't hear me," he continues. "You ran right out of the class before I had a chance to talk to you." His smile is thin. "You did a great job today. I saw your stacks of gold."

"Yeah. It wasn't—" hard. No, I can't say that to him. Not when he struggled. A tutor. The great Theo Acaster needs a tutor for his classes. I can't wrap my mind around the concept.

He's breathtaking, so alive and in charge, even more so now than before. That's the only thought circling inside my head. From the cut of his shoulders to the squareness of his jaw and the slightly off-center bend of his nose, as though it's been broken before.

I see with absolute certainty why Theo Acaster is the king of this school.

What I don't understand is how he's so close to failing out. I know sometimes it's hard for people to marry concepts and execution. I'm a bookworm, a nerd, so that's my forte. Theo seems to be much better at dealing with the people around him than abstracts. It's a strength.

"I know we've never spoken—" he begins.

Understatement of the century.

"—but I want to ask you a question."

He nudges me to get me to start walking. It doesn't seem as though there's any direction in mind which is better for me. I'm barely able to concentrate as it is with him right there next to me.

"You can ask me anything," I reply.

A little too eagerly, in my opinion, but Theo stares ahead, too lost in his head to notice.

"Would you be willing to tutor me? You never have a problem in classes. In fact, you're the only witch I know who manages to get through each assignment without a single hiccup." He rushes to get through the statement and since his face gives nothing away, I have to wonder why. "What you do is admirable no matter what the others say."

Immediately my heart leaps to thud against my ribs and demands I tell him yes.

It would be an opportunity to get close to him, it reasons. To show him the real me. To win his affection.

My brain forces my heart to reel it in.

"You saw me?" I ask instead.

He nods slowly. "You're a little hard to miss."

I blush again, wondering if he'd say the same if he saw me in my street clothes rather than the school uniform. "Here I thought…never mind what I thought."

"Apparently," he continues with forced lightness, "and as I'm sure you already know since you see everything, I'm not doing as well in classes as I might be. To the point where I'm close to flunking out if I can't make it through the next round of tests. They're coming up."

"And you want me to tutor you?" I repeat, like saying it out loud with my own mouth makes it real.

"I'd like that, yes."

Yes, say yes. My heart begs me. What comes out instead is, "Sorry, I have enough problems."

In fact, several of them approach as we speak.

A glance at the building ahead shows me several girls who must have been waiting for him to get to his next class. There are Courtney and Kimberly, although Helena doesn't seem to be in their midst. They gather in a pack and although they offer smiles to his back, for me, it's thunderclouds.

A clear question as to what the hell someone like Theo is doing with me.

I'm asking myself the same question.

"You're right, I notice things. Helping you is going to put a bigger target on my back than is already painted there." I stop a split second away from smacking myself in the forehead at my bluntness. "I'm not sure why I told you that. Suffice it to say, there are better people out there to tutor you. People who are more on your level in terms of social status."

Not to mention actual tutors. Or an upperclassman.

"What if I told you I know of something that can fix both our problems?" Theo offers. "I had a little time to think about it when you bolted out of the classroom."

He's not backing down.

"I'd say you have my curiosity piqued." I wrap my arms around my midsection, holding tightly to keep myself from splintering in a thousand different directions.

"We don't really have a lot of time to talk right now, considering our audience." Theo stops and steps in front of me to get me to hear him out, blocking me with his body. "It really is the best solution for both of us, Yasmine."

There he goes, saying my name again.

"I'd say that's a hell of a proposition," I squeak out. "I'm also not buying it."

"You should meet me tonight. Before curfew, of course, at the Merlin statue at the center of campus." He adjusts the strap of his bag over his shoulder, hair flopping into his eyes like one of the guys on Blaire's boy-band posters, and my heart stutters. "You've seen the monument, I'm sure."

Not beseeching me to consider his offer this time, either.

"Who?" I ask.

"Okay, so it's not really Merlin. Everyone calls the statue that but it's really just an unknown witch who founded the place." Theo turns up the heat on his grin. "What do you say? Please say you'll consider hearing me out."

I say I'm sunk.

I say I'm a goner.

I say I'm the world's biggest idiot.

And what comes out of my mouth sounds suspiciously like, "Yes."

CHAPTER
TWELVE

I float solidly on cloud nine for the rest of the day because the boy of my dreams knows my name. He wants to meet me. He wants me to tutor him.

Me, not Helena. Not any of the other girls who want to hang off his arm.

I manage to get through the rest of my classes wondering the entire time what Theo's offer might be. It's one thing to want him to know my name. But now? To even consider meeting with him after dark?

I'm asking to get jumped on the way there.

The looks his groupies shot me when I hurried off to the dorm had been both maddening and frightening at the same time. If one of them met me alone on the green?

I'm not sure who would make it out of the encounter.

Not to mention all the other things that take place after dark. If I don't stop thinking about romance, I'll be setting myself up for disappointment and getting severely ahead of myself.

What had Mom always said?

I need to stay grounded in *this* reality and not the one I want to create.

The one where Theo learns he just can't live without me and we're together forever.

My first real crush, I think as I hustle to get cleaned up after dinner.

No wonder I'm getting carried away.

Basically, wishes aren't going to get me anywhere far and it's not good to lose myself in fantasies. I always took Mom's warnings about daydreams with a grain of salt but this time, she's totally right. Theo is a fantasy. The two of us together? The absolute opposite of reality and he only wants to meet me for help.

Case closed.

Shortly before curfew, making excuses to Blaire about needing a breath of air and a walk, I make my way toward the monument at the center of campus.

I've passed the statue a number of times but never really given it much thought until tonight.

I spot Theo waiting for me at the base of the statue, pacing. He runs his hands through his auburn hair and his steps kick up a fair amount of dust from the ground.

He's been at it for a while.

What's going on in his mind right now?

It's pointless to wonder, just like there's no telling why he's getting behind in his classes when he struck me as intelligent.

I really don't know much about him besides

whatever I've picked up through the rumor mill and from Blaire. The usual stuff. Like the fact that Theo is the first-born son of his family and the position puts a lot of pressure on him to do well.

Like he has to succeed in the face of everything.

Doesn't everyone have some kind of problem? Well, unless the person is me and my very small, tiny problem regarding the still ongoing criminal investigation.

The thought is enough to stop me in my tracks a few paces away. My stomach drops and my mouth goes dry. He won't want to be anywhere near me if he finds out about the arson, and my inability to control myself.

Theo sees me while I'm still lost in my head and his frantic pacing stops at the same time his face splits in a smile. This is a completely different side of him and nothing I've seen before. Not directed at me, anyway.

The smile lights him from the inside out and changes the entire set of his features.

"You actually showed up," he calls out.

Unless I miss my mark, he sounds…happy. *Elated* is pushing it but *joyful* is not much of a stretch.

"Yeah, I did," I say, a little embarrassed, holding my elbow to keep myself contained.

My feet skid on my next few steps and I'm not sure how to fight against a large part of me that wants to rush over and leap into his arms, kiss him stupid.

The seconds stretch on until I'm right in front of him with blinders on for the rest of the world. Everything narrows until it's us, the statue, the thumping of my heart. It all melts away until there's only Theo because he's looking at me. He's giving me his full attention and it feels both strange and wonderful at the same time.

"So, what's this plan of yours?" I ask in a desperate bid to fill the empty space between us with words. "You said you have a way to help us both. Let's hear it."

"So eager," he purrs. *Oh, god*. My cheeks burst into flame. "I certainly think this will help us both." He smiles at me and my knees melt. "It's no secret you've had a hard time."

I scoff. "Define hard time."

He's nothing but sympathy and understanding as he says, "You might not have seen me, but you're impossible not to notice, Yasmine. You've had some trouble finding your footing since you came. Not with classes, but with the rest of the academy experience."

"Um." My insides feel hot and uncomfortable. "Well, it hasn't been the easiest," I admit, so embarrassed I'm lightheaded. My entire body is so hot it's impossible to tell if he actually sees me blushing in the dark or not. "It's not a simple thing to come into school in the middle of the semester."

"You excel in your classes, though," Theo insists. "You always know the right answer and you're done with your practices before everyone else."

"I'm well read." I'm also squirming.

"Exactly my point, and I need a tutor. Which leads me to my proposition." He leans back against the statue with his arms crossed over his chest. "I need help. You need help in a different way."

I eye him, waiting for him to continue.

"Fitting in," he clarifies. "You're not having the best

time making friends. That's one thing I know how to do. I'll be your fake plus one for this semester. *If* you can help me pass my classes."

He lets those final words settle and it takes me more than a few seconds to realize the implications.

A fake plus one? He wants to pretend to be my... friend. Date? No, impossible.

"I'm not going to cheat for you just to make sure you stay in class, if that's the kind of help you're asking for. That's not...it's not okay." I'm fumbling over my words like an idiot. "I don't cheat. And I don't need help making friends."

Theo chuckles, the sound is dark and rich and straight out of my wildest dreams. What choice do I have but to swoon? I hide the movement by shifting to his side and leaning my hip on the base of the statue.

"I don't want to cheat," Theo corrects. "I need someone to make sure I know the material. For some reason, directions and execution don't mesh for me. I can't become a high priest if someone else is doing the work for me." He runs a hand through his hair once again, the strands already messed from before, and the movement captivates me. Then, dropping his voice low to avoid being overheard by anyone nearby, he admits, "None of this stuff really makes sense to me. Ever. I've always had an issue with this kind of thing and right now, when it counts the most, I can't make it work on my own."

I nod along with the words. I understand.

Sometimes it's hard to follow along, especially if you

have questions from the start. It can make the rest of the spellwork seem incomprehensible.

He doesn't want me to cheat. That's a relief.

But...

"Let me see if I'm following," I start. "You want me to tutor you in the source material and in return...what? You'll pretend you're interested in me?" I shake my head. "I feel pathetic enough as it is. I don't need your pity."

How humiliating. I want to tell him no. I might have some problems socially but that doesn't mean I need someone to pretend for me, to pity me.

Besides, what about Helena?

I say none of these things as I work my way through the scenario in my head.

"There's no pity involved." Theo shifts a little closer and his scent hits me like a brick to the side of the face. Wow, he smells good. Earthy and spicy and a hint of sweat. "Believe me, Yasmine."

"You don't know me."

"You're right, I don't. I know what I see and it's enough for me. We can help each other." He flashes me a smile, the wattage dim, as though he's not sure he's getting through to me. "If you agree."

A glance down at my watch has my eyes bulging. "Look, if I don't make it back to the dorm then there's going to be hell to pay. It's almost curfew. And I need to think about this." I shake my head. I can't make a decision on the spot. There are a lot of things to consider before blindly entering into any agreement, even if the agreement is with the man of my dreams.

"I get it," Theo says, and he sounds calm. Easy. No skin off his back when I'm reeling on the inside. I turn to leave as he trots to my side. "I'll walk you back."

"You want to walk together?" I blanch. "People will see us."

"So what? There's nothing for you to worry about. Even if you're late back to your dorm. You're with me."

He doesn't sound nearly as haughty as he might have been making the statement. His attention on the path ahead of us, Theo walks with long confident strides and his shoulders squared. There's no hint of the jerk I saw in the cafeteria on my first day.

No hint of his usual impish grin, either. Any mischief has dimmed along with the smile. Why?

"You understand that no one will ever believe that we're together," I blurt out. *Cute.* "If I agree to do this thing with you, that is. No one will think you're interested in me. Heck, *I* don't even believe it, and I'm standing next to you. We don't go together."

He stares sideways at me. "You let me worry about that. I'm very good at being convincing when I don't feel a certain way. I've had a lot of practice there, too."

I gnaw on that nugget of truth from him on the entire trek back to my dorm. And despite the late hour and the nearing curfew, there are still people milling around. Eyes fall on me, on Theo, then right back to me with such potency I feel it like a physical touch.

We stop in front of the door to X House and stand facing each other. "Well, thanks for walking me back. I'll give some thought to your...proposal." What else is there to say? "I'm not sure I agree with it but…maybe I can help you."

I'm still not entirely sold despite wanting to leap ahead with eyes closed and not knowing how things are going to go down.

Theo leans forward, tucking a loose strand of hair behind my ear. I freeze at the contact. "That's all I'm asking. I'll see you tomorrow, Yas. Let me know what you decide."

I stand there with my lips parted slightly and watch him walk away. I can feel my cheeks heating up. *Yas*. He called me Yas.

With a squeak of surprise, I turn and hurry toward the door. Then, because I'm curious, I turn back just in time to see him looking at me with a grin.

A besotted grin.

Ohhhhh my gosh!

Making it back to my room just in time for the bells to chime and signal curfew, I lean against the door focusing on my breathing. If that little interaction proves anything to me, it's that his plan might just work.

Anyone looking at him would see exactly what he wants them to see. That he likes me. That we're together.

Wow.

Now I just need to give him his answer tomorrow.

There is much more to Theo than meets the eye and, despite wanting to figure him out, first thing's first: how do we make this work without me falling hard?

CHAPTER
THIRTEEN

Blaire is already up and gone by the time I wake up in the morning. Her bag with all her books isn't in its usual heap beside the desk. In this room, though, I'm never alone. There are a thousand eyes watching at any given moment. Luckily for me, I'm used to them.

Last night's dreams had been a slideshow of reality interwoven with fiction, memories of Theo touching me and where else he might touch. He wore a kilt for the last half of my dreams.

A highland Theo is sexier than anything else.

What am I going to do about him?

I know I can help him with his grades. If Mom taught me anything, it's the importance of rigidity and schedule when it comes to studying. I know I can help him through the source material in a way he'll understand. As for his half of the bargain…it still seems a little like pity to me. Him pretending to be my friend, my date.

I know I'm right about one thing: no one is going to believe we're together.

I swing my legs over the side of the bed, feet on the cold wooden floor.

Gus scurries from his hiding spot, up my arm, to perch on my shoulder. Already alert with his whiskers twitching and his eyes on some point across the room.

"What's the matter?" I ask.

The protection spell is wearing off, he says. *You've got to spell another one before you go to class today. There's something looming. I'm not sure what it is.*

"You feel it?"

Don't you?

Looming—I don't like the sound of that.

Taking a second when I want to panic, I tune into the energies of the room and my own intuition. I don't feel what he does but if Gus is worried enough to tell me, then it's best to be on my guard and aware today.

Understanding his concern, I make quick work redoing the protection spell and his cold nose presses on my cheek.

"Thanks," I say out loud. "You're the best. What would I do without you?"

Suffer? I'm not sure.

He's always looking out for me, watching and making sure I'm cared for. I don't know what I'd do without him.

With the protection spell back in place, I stand in front of the closet to grab a clean uniform.

"You know what today feels like?" I ask Gus. I hold the hanger with my blazer out in front of me. It's a step up from granny chic but not by much. "It feels like it's time for a makeover."

You've made the decision already, huh?

"It's been a long time coming, too. Remi had been hounding me for years about dressing my age. I've already made up my mind. Everyone wears a uniform here. The basic look can remain the same but maybe I can spruce up the rest of things."

And look a little more like the girl who might actually draw the attention of a guy like Theo. Not that there's anything wrong with me and the way I look.

It's past time. I've been thinking about a makeover since Blaire started telling me about her transformation magic. How the women she helped in the past told her she worked wonders. How much better would I feel, about myself, about being here, if I was confident in my outward appearance?

The saying is to dress for success.

I've dressed like a hermit.

There's no reason to own anything nice when you work in a library. I never got out and I never saw anyone besides the coven members. Mom made sure to keep me isolated from the rest of the community, and loving books the way I do, escaping into them, I never minded. Much.

Now everything is different.

The only dress code was work casual at the library and the only people who saw me on any daily basis were Mom and Remi.

Being here might be a kind of imposed exile but

there is no reason for me to not make the most of it, which starts with my appearance.

I glance at my watch. I've got just enough time to hit the campus store. I've always seen Remi wearing cherry lip gloss. She'd smack it across her lips, shoot me a smile, and go on with her day like she's about to take over the world. Maybe that's what I need, too.

It's a small start, but it's definitely a start.

"Stay here and hide," I tell Gus. "I'll be right back."

You want to change out of your pajamas first? He laughs at me as I shake a leg, literally, staring down at my navy-blue pajama pants dotted with little polar bears.

"Yeah, it might be helpful."

A few minutes later, I'm on my way to the campus store.

It's not a huge space but I know they have a few toiletry items and makeup pieces in the back. Heading in that general direction, I force a smile on my face. Even when I overhear two girls chatting over a row of water bottles.

"Can you even believe it?" the first hisses out. "He dropped her off at the misfit house. He was, like, touching her. Smiling and shit."

"I know, it's such a shame," the other commiserates. "All that gorgeousness wasted on someone like her. When Helena finds out Theo is slumming it, she is going to flip out!"

"It's not a shame. It's absolute BS!" the first insists.

The second snorts dismissively. "How do you know it's BS?"

"Because someone like him *would not* be seen with a

girl like her. Let alone actually be interested in her." Now the first one scoffs, the sound wet and awful. "It's ridiculous. She is the social equivalent of poison. Anyone seen with her is asking to be isolated."

It's none of my business what they're saying. They're gossips. I'm prepared to ignore them both until I hear my name.

"Yasmine and *Theo?*"

My fingers still on a wand of mascara, and I snag a look at her in the mirror overhead, the reflection is of the two blondes bent together. And they're taking no pains to keep their thoughts to themselves.

"She must have put a hex on him in order to do her will. He's under her spell and has no choice but to do her bidding, the poor thing." One of them clucks their tongue. "It's the only way this makes sense."

Shit. This is not a consequence I've considered, and it makes me even more hesitant to accept his offer if *this* is the immediate reaction of people around us. It isn't enough for us to have to maintain a ruse of dating. Now we have to prove there's no magic involved.

I grab the mascara and some kind of lip gloss, probably not cherry flavored, and bolt to the front of the store to pay.

Makeover be damned.

I've got to do a lot of thinking this morning and a coat of gloss isn't going to help me make the right decision.

I told Theo this wouldn't work, I think to myself on my way back to the dorm. Or if I hadn't actually said it out loud then I wanted to.

It seems to me there is more to lose than there is to gain but I'm not sure if I'll ever get a chance to get to know Theo again. Is a potential friendship between us, outside of fake dating, even possible?

If I say no to tutoring him, I'll never find out.

He's worth it, though, isn't he? Having the chance to be around Theo and get to know him has to be worth more than empty words from two unremarkable witches.

Getting to know him *and* exploring my first real crush. It's a chance I have to take. Even if I have to face the blowback.

By the time I make it back to the dorm, I've already made up my mind to go through with this. I'll tutor him, and he'll…fake date me. *I guess*. It's a little too late for us to decide on another course of action because tongues are already wagging just from him dropping me off last night.

It makes me feel a little weird inside.

Which means I've got to take action to prove a relationship between us is not only possible but happening at this moment. It's up to me to sell the lie, too, not just Theo.

At least I've made it out of the store before the girls see me. Theo hasn't given me his number, waiting for me to come to him to either agree or back out, so I've got to find him based on his schedule. And I totally know his schedule.

What can I say?

He's my crush.

I stand beside the bushes outside of his dorm

waiting for him to leave for his morning class in the astrology building. The lip gloss burns a hole in my pocket and I feel absolutely foolish for thinking it would make any kind of difference in the first place.

If Remi was here, she'd mock me up one side and down the other.

After a few tense seconds, Theo steps through the front doors and I throw a pebble at him. "Psst!" It's way louder than I thought but the noise does the trick and gets his attention. "Over here."

He cranes his head to the side, confused, until he sees me and rolls his eyes. "What are you doing in the bushes? Come on, Yas, that's silly."

Feeling ridiculous, I straighten and step out. "I'm waiting for you. We need to talk," I say. "I, ah, have an answer for you."

"If you know my dorm then you could have just come up to my room. It's 129. Or you could have called." He points behind him to a doorbell with one copper colored brow arched. "You push in the room number and it sends a signal up to me."

"Well, I didn't have your number, and this is important."

He chuckles and holds out a hand for me to help me even further out of the bush. "You've got shit all over you. The bushes, seriously?" Deft fingers remove a few stray twigs from my hair.

And his hands linger a bit along the line of my jaw.

"You want to talk about last night?" he asks softly. "You have an answer for me?"

I nod, gnawing on my lower lip. Why is this so hard

to get out? "I was thinking about your proposal. And I think we can make it work, but the only way for this to work is if people know I haven't put a spell or a hex on you." I shift in discomfort. "I actually heard two girls at the campus store talking about it just now."

"Talking about you? Putting a spell on me?" Theo chuckles again, biting back from outright laughing, his face tilted to the sky. Finally he says, "Somehow it always surprises me how quickly news travels, good or bad. There are always eyes on me."

Yeah, which worries me on a deep level. "No one is going to buy us as a couple if we can't prove that magic is not involved. They see I'm totally beneath you." He's standing in my breathing space, close enough for me to reach out and touch, and for some reason the pulse of his heartbeat in his neck has me in a thrall.

"Hey, no." Theo reaches out to take me by the shoulders and lightly shake. "You're *not* beneath me. You're overthinking things. This arrangement is between you and me, and as long as we have each other's backs, then nothing else matters." He sounds strong and assured, the way I've wanted to feel and somehow found too far a reach. "We can overcome any bad bridges later."

Sure, *later* sounds good.

Later sounds doable because right now things feel a little too tense and prickly for my liking.

"If you're good to say yes, then I'm all in, Yas. Starting now. You want it to be believable?" He shifts his hands down along the line of my arms, links his fingers through mine to hold my hand. "I need you."

He needs me.

Well, poo. It's the one thing he can say that is guaranteed to burrow beneath my skin and lodge there. Right above my heart and spreading out through every corner of my body. Theo needs me. And right now, I don't want to stop and think about all the other people at the school who are so much better equipped to tutor him. Or what people will say when we're together.

I look into his eyes, the color deep and rich and swoon-worthy, and I melt.

No matter how afraid I am of what's going to happen.

"Okay, fine," I finally agree. "Yes. We're doing this."

His face breaks out in a wide grin and I find my own expression shifting to match it as he squeezes my hand. "That's great. I'm really glad you agreed. Really glad."

I have no idea why and I'm done trying to understand. I swallow the girlish giggle wanting to erupt. "Great." I tuck a lock of hair behind my ear, remembering Theo doing the same for me last night, and I break out in hives.

Metaphorically speaking.

The way my face burns, though, I'm definitely blushing again. I hope it's not going to be a regular occurrence.

"Let me walk you to class," he says. "We might as well start this deal off right. Are you free later?" His arm winds around my shoulder and he tugs me close. My insides go right up in flames. "I want to start tutoring as soon as possible, especially with tests coming up."

I yelp out something affirmative at his excitement.

I'm not capable of real words at this point.

Because Theo is touching me, and there is no mistaking his possessiveness. Or his public display of the two of us together. My muscles tense. I'm not relaxed at all.

Which of course, Theo notices.

"Yas, you're going to have to calm down," he tells me. "You're as stiff as a board. I'm sure you've walked like this with one of your exes."

"I don't have exes."

I want to slap myself. Why did I say something so pathetic?

"Come on, Yas, I'm sure you've had them lining up down the street for you." Theo doesn't believe me.

I'm also unable to touch him back even when my arm is itching to shift to his waist. To land there. Already the heat of him seeps into me.

"How about you talk to me? Tell me something about yourself that no one knows. Something you've never told anyone," he presses. "No lies."

Except coming from him it doesn't sound pushy at all. It sounds like the best invitation I've had to be open and vulnerable in my life. Trusting him might not be the smartest idea, however.

Especially since the first thing that comes to mind, something I've never told anyone, happens to involve a freaky grimoire and a horned god. Or even the fire at the library. If anyone were to find out about those things, it could ruin my new start.

No, those secrets will have to wait for another time, and maybe another person. This is just a ruse. I have to remind myself of that. A ruse that requires boundaries in place for my safety.

"I'm just not used to any kinds of public displays of affection," I say by way of explanation. "It might be normal for you, but this is my first actual—" I cut off the words just starting to come out of my mouth. Being out of my depth does strange things. "Especially since I thought that you...you and Helena were together."

I stop before I put my foot in my mouth further and Theo chuckles in the silence.

"Helena likes to think there's more going on than there actually is, especially since we called it off at the start of the semester," he fills in. "She's not someone you need to worry about. I'm sure you've heard about us. We've been on and off for years, before even coming to Andora. This time the breakup is permanent."

"It's a relief for sure, but it doesn't help me feel any more at ease."

We've fallen into step beside each other in an easy rhythm, my strides lengthening to keep up with him.

"If you're worried about her being jealous, don't be." His voice hardens. "She's all bark and no bite, if she decides to make a big deal at all. It's just you and me right now, Yas," he adds. "For this to work, we've got to sell it. I know you're going to do your part because you're the smartest person here. No doubt. Smart enough to be able to play along with this."

Suddenly we're at the door to my next class and Theo removes his arm from around my shoulder and sets me with a loaded, intentional look.

"I'll see you later. Come to my room after dinner and we'll get started," he says. "Okay? We'll go from there."

What have I done?

I watch him walk off with a whistle on his lips, my legs doing the dirty work for me and bringing me into the classroom. I grab a seat next to Blaire.

She's gaping at me, her eyes wide enough for me to lose sight of her eyebrows in the pink fringe of her bangs. "Did I seriously see you and Theo together? With his arm around you?" she starts, incredulous. I don't even have a chance to nod before she's forging ahead with, "How? When? What? Why?"

The situation is so insane I giggle in response, shrugging.

"You've somehow gone from public enemy number one to landing the hottest guy on campus!" She taps her fingers on her chin. "This is amazing."

"The word you're looking for is weird. Strange. Miraculous." Do I tell her about the deal?

"We need to up your game," Blaire decides. "Absolutely step number one in whatever is going on… we take you from drab to fab."

"I have no game to up!"

"Every girl within five miles knows about Theo and what a catch he really is. Not just his good looks, but his status, his family, the whole bit, Yazzy. Girls throw themselves at him all the time! We need you to stand out if you have any hope of keeping him past the end of the week," she continues. Her eyes brighten. "Yes, that's exactly what we need. I'm the one who can help you."

Nope, there's no way I'm telling her about the deal

we made together. Not when she's looking at me like I'm finally someone worth knowing, like she placed her bet on the right horse after all. And since Blaire is my only real friend on this campus because I'm not ready to count Theo yet, I want to let her help.

Blaire has always been great. But things have changed in an instant between us on a whole other level. Now I'm not such a hopeless case.

"Yes," she says to answer herself. "Tonight, after class, we're doing a makeover."

"I can't tonight. I'm meeting Theo in his room," I reply. Ready to hysterical giggle again when her eyes bulge a second time. "And have you ever thought that maybe he likes me for me? I mean, it's not such a stretch. Is it?"

Blaire speaks to me, her finger doing half of the explaining for her, like I am a child who needs a little extra guidance. "It's not about you, really. Men eat with their imaginations. They are visual creatures. You want to whet his appetite. Sure, Yazzy, you landed him. Now it's time to keep him. Long term." She points a warning finger at me. "That's what you want, isn't it? You're not going to be one of those girls who gets used and discarded. I won't let it happen! You feel me?"

The professor calls for attention, putting an end to our conversation. I glance out the window just in time to catch sight of a shadow moving into the nearby trees.

This time, I know it's not just my imagination.

The shadow is real, and shifts just out of my field of vision the moment I notice it.

My hands tingle.

Something about the situation isn't right. Something about the darkness of the shadow and the way my body automatically reacts has me catching my breath.

I hide them in my lap even though it does no good. The sensation persists.

CHAPTER
FOURTEEN

I t's hard to hold a wand with my hands.
    Even harder to execute the simple spells the professor requires.

Blaire keeps staring at me, wanting to know what the hell is wrong as I fumble in a way I never have before.

The shadow.

I watch out the window like a hawk stalking prey, except in this case, I'm not the predator. Not even close.

There's something out there, and a sinking sensation in my gut tells me it's been here the whole time, I've just been too distracted to notice. Whether it really is the Horned God or not is impossible to say without seeing him. I try tuning into my intuition and come up with zilch.

"Miss Williams! You need to focus," the professor admonishes when I drop my wand for the hundredth time.

My mind is a blur of everything that's happened and

the anxiety caused by my tingling hands. The shadow doesn't return but now I know I'm not making things up or seeing things out of fear.

Torn between worry for what it means, wondering about the shadow, and the strangeness of this agreement with Theo, it's a wonder I even manage to answer the ten questions on our random pop quiz on crystal usages.

Class ends, and Theo is outside the door waiting for me. He looks up from his feet, his face lighting and his lips spreading in a slow grin designed to melt hearts.

My stomach flips at the sight of him and Blaire is suddenly there beside me. She stares him up and down appraisingly.

"Ah, Blaire, this is Theo. Theo, this is my roommate and friend, Blaire," I say in introduction.

From the way she's always spoken about him, I know they're not actually acquainted.

"Actually, I think we have Latin together. I know I've seen you before." He smiles at her outfit. "You stand out." He's charming. Polite. "It's a pleasure to finally meet such a talented witch. Transformation magic is something special."

His charms work on everyone, I see. Blaire, who is always so self-composed, now has twin dots of rose on her cheeks. "We have several classes together, actually. Not just Latin." Her voice comes out breathless. "Yasmine is a great girl, Theo. You should be forever grateful she's looked your way."

"I know." He doesn't pause for even a moment before saying, "You have nothing to worry about. I'm sure this seems a little fast, but I like Yas, too. I want her to be happy. I know I'm the guy who can make her happy."

If he'd so much as followed the statement with a wink, he wouldn't have sold it with quite the same level of success.

As it is, he looks honest. As though he really is interested in me, for some reason, enough to sell it to Blaire, and me, and anyone else who walks by and sees us.

Damn me.

Damn him because when he looks at me, when he smiles, even I believe him and I know the deal between us. I know exactly what's going on between us and I'm falling under his spell regardless.

"How about you join us for lunch? It will give us a chance to hang out and get a little more comfortable with each other," Theo offers.

It's an olive branch and we all understand it. Blaire only takes a moment to consider before saying yes.

Until she meets my eyes and I shake my head. "We can't, I'm sorry." I wiggle my eyebrows to try and remind Blaire what we have to do over lunch. When she fails to pick up the hint, I say, "Blaire and I have something planned. A surprise. For you, actually."

Theo blinks at me. "I love surprises."

"This is going to be a good one." Feeling bold, I loop my arm through his and bump against him suggestively. "I hope you'll like it."

"I'm sure I will. I'll see you later." He leans over, whispering the statement in my ear, and I shiver.

Together, I stand alongside Blaire as Theo says his goodbyes and heads back down the hallway.

"I cannot believe it," Blaire says under her breath. "And if I hadn't seen it for myself then I'd call you a liar but there he was, looking at you like he wanted to gobble you up."

"Whole," I agreed without hesitation. "You're right."

"Now what are we doing that's so important I'm missing—shit, girl." A grin broke out across her face. "Your makeover because you have plans tonight. I am so dense. His gorgeousness blinded me." She taps the side of her head.

"His gorgeousness is a weapon," I agree.

She pulls me out of the building toward our room and I pause, glancing around the open campus. Only normal shadows.

My hands tingle, a reminder of what I've seen.

But there's nothing out here now.

It doesn't stop me from watching everything the rest of the way toward our room. Blaire sits me down in *her* usual chair, running her hands through my short hair.

"You've got some natural good looks. I mean, this skin tone." She blows a chef's kiss. "It's pure gold, Yazzy. You can do a lot with it if you believe in yourself."

"You're asking for a lot," I tell her.

"I don't think I am. You know, I think you should rock it even shorter." Her fingertips trail from my ears down to the planes of my cheeks and my jaw. "You've got the angles for a chin length cut, and I know you don't want to hear it, but the shorter hair is going to leave more of your face open. These eyes of yours…

they're big and expressive. You need to show them off."

It had sounded like such a great idea when she mentioned the makeover in class. Now, facing the reality of changing my looks…

"I've always had long hair," I reveal. "I feel naked without mine. Witches are supposed to have long glorious locks. That kind of thing."

Blaire sucks on her teeth. "Not modern witches. It's not going to take much but I've got a great canvas I'm working with. Do you trust me?"

No. I automatically want to tell her no. Rather than disagree, I swallow and nod. Once. "Do whatever you want to do. But please don't cut it any shorter."

I hope I won't regret giving her the green light.

"Fine, I'll clean it up." She squeezes my shoulders reassuringly. "I've got you."

Blaire gets to work, and the changes are small, at first. Or so she tells me. Things like cleaning up my eyebrows, slapping on a face mask while she gives me a trim. She keeps me away from the mirror until she's done, slathering on a coat of copper eyeshadow and a darker shade along my crease.

"I've only revealed what's already there, you know. Your natural beauty," she tells me when she's done. "No magic required." She reaches for her small handheld mirror and holds it out for me. "Take a look."

My stomach drops in the best way.

The woman looking back at me from the reflection is me, but so much more. It's as though Blaire elevated my usual looks to the complete next level. Not only does the new haircut compliment my face, but my eyes are huge with the mascara and the eyeshadow she applied. My lips are slicked with a pretty floral color that brings out the blush of my cheeks, which she emphasized.

"I can't believe it," I murmur.

She gives me a small, tight hug. "Theo will not let you out of his sight once he sees you now. Not that looks are the most important thing in a relationship, but you're drop dead, and you deserve to feel confident, which people naturally do when they look good. He's going to be all over you," she finishes.

All over me…

My mind flashes back to the dreams of last night and the things we did together. The hysterical giggles are back. "I'm not too sure I like the idea." I bite down on my lower lip to keep them contained. "I, ah, feel foolish even saying this."

"Go ahead, girl. This is a no judgment zone."

"All I know about romance I learned from reading books about hot Scots in the highland. And Theo doesn't wear a kilt," I say. "Not outside of dreams."

Plus, this is all pretend.

I just need to make sure I play a convincing part.

"What do you mean, you only know about romance from books?" Blaire says. "Are you seriously telling me you've never dated before?"

God, having to admit it to two people in one day? The secret I've carried for so long?

I blink at my reflection but the deer in the headlights look doesn't work with my makeover.

"I've never dated before." I wince saying it out loud, covering my face with my hands until Blaire slaps them away. "I've never gone out with a boy or held his hand. Until now. I've been homeschooled since I learned how to speak." Once it's out in the open, it's much easier to say without getting tongue tied.

"But you're so cute. And you're smart!" Blaire exclaims. "How were you living like a monk?"

"Easily. It's all I've ever known."

Right now, it's a source of embarrassment.

I've never had a chance to live. I'm supposed to be at Andora to learn about magic, but what about the rest of it? The social things that make life worth living?

Those had never been available to me until now.

Blaire taps her finger on the top of my still tingling hand before grabbing my chair and pulling it over so that we're facing each other, leaving me no choice but to face her head on. "You've been really close lipped about your background," she replies cautiously, afraid to spook me. "I get it. Sometimes it's hard to talk about our pasts, especially when we don't trust anyone. But I'm your friend, Yazzy. You can talk to me about anything. And lord knows my life is an open book. Any question you want is on the table. I'd just like to know more about you."

I take a second because all of a sudden it's hard to breathe with my feelings rising up out of the boxes where I smashed them. Too many and all varied, making it hard to figure them out and deal with them. Which was probably why I hadn't until now.

"It's not going to be the best story." It's the only warning I offer.

She bobs her head in a nod. "I get it. Try me."

"I'm on the outs with my family," I finally tell Blaire. "We're not supposed to speak with each other. I really miss my sister." I glance at her. "You actually remind me a lot of Remi. She's older and she's always been more confident. So sure of herself and unafraid."

"Time heals all wounds," Blaire says. Her way of letting me know I don't need to get it all out in the open right away. "You've been here a few weeks. And the semester is only halfway through! Maybe you can go and see them during the break. It's coming up."

"I don't think I'm allowed to see them," I admit. "My mother said some things to me as she dropped me off. It's not really easy, even if I want to."

"If anyone is able to figure this out, it's you. I think you need to channel some of your sister's badass energy, maybe even some of mine, at the risk of sounding like I have a big head. Channel it, own it, and start thinking about what you really want. Not what other people want for you."

A grin tweaks my cheeks up. "Has anyone ever told you that you give good advice?"

Blaire fluffs her hair. "It's my gift."

I don't want to think about a visit, however. Planning this ruse, helping Theo, figuring myself out… deciding what I might do during break is way more than I want to contend with. And I'm at capacity.

CHAPTER
FIFTEEN

After a very early dinner, I head over to Theo's dorm, watching every step.

If there are creatures out there, or more fog, then I need to be observant. My hands stopped tingling halfway through our meal. A blessing, thank goodness, but a new tingle took up residence in my lower abdomen at the thought of where I'm heading.

Despite the squirming in my guts, I head up to his room.

No more strange shadows separate from the darkness. A normal breeze pushes the leaves of the trees overhead in a sweet symphony, along with my pounding footsteps. Pounding everything, really. I'm the one who's out of place, abnormal, coming from X House, thinking a layer of makeup will protect me.

My self-critic never shuts up, and whatever is lurking out there has not given up.

Maybe it's just hibernating for a bit.

Is Theo going to like my new look?

How much studying am I going to be able to get done with my nerves raw and on edge?

I force myself to knock on his door even when my heart pounds out of my chest to the point where my ribs ache. I'm breathless again, the way I always seem to be around him.

I've got no control.

And it's different this time because this is my life. I'm not in the pages of my stories faced with a ruggedly handsome fictional man. I'm with Theo Acaster.

Or I'm about to be.

Guys walk along the hallway and stare at me. The attention only intensifies my breathing. This isn't natural, the way they look at me. And it's not even bad attention, as their smiles are appreciative. Curious. Open in a way they've never been before when most people's attention either tends to skip over me or snag in a bad way.

Open the door, Theo.

Gus gave me a pep talk on my way over and everything goes out the window a second later, my unspoken plea answered when the door swings open. And every ounce of moisture in my mouth dries up because Theo is bare chested. A towel hangs around his neck with sweat dripping from his brow.

I know better than to gawk but damn. Hot, *hot* damn.

"Hey, Yas. Come on in." He steps aside to let me enter. "I just finished playing basketball and I didn't know you'd be over so early. Sorry I'm not prepared."

I can barely speak. How is this going to work if I

have no control when I see him? I have to stop being weird.

I definitely stare at his chest way longer than I should because he's glorious. So hot and masculine and absolutely built. He's got just enough muscles on his lanky form to show he keeps in shape without getting too bulky for his frame.

"If you don't mind, I'm going to rinse off and get changed," he says, pausing at the door. "Make yourself comfortable. I'll be right back."

I nod, my mouth hanging open slightly until he's out of the room and I feel like I can actually draw air into my lungs.

I'm alone in Theo's room.

It's a dream come true and a nightmare at the same time because I'm not supposed to be here. Except he says he needs me and even though I have a hard time believing him, I know I need him more. Even if he hadn't proposed this ruse of ours, I'd still need him, because there was something about him. There's no chance I'm walking away.

While he's gone, though…

I can breathe better once he's out of the room. This is the spot I've thought about most often, his inner sanctum. What kind of personal effects has he brought with him from home to make this space feel comfortable?

The first things I look for are memorabilia pertaining to his relationship with Helena. I find none. No pictures of the two of them or indication that any woman has been in this room for a while. His roommate's bed is made and fastidiously neat, along with the rest of that side of the room.

I walk over to Theo's desk and trail my hands along the spines of the books he has piled there. He never struck me as the type to lose himself in them. Not like me.

Theo is the opposite of me.

He's everyone's friend, the guy who offers a smile easily to whoever is around. He's the social butterfly and the Golden Boy of the school.

But he reads, for fun. Not all of them are required reading for class, although a lot of them are, but he's got a few historical biographies peppered in. A couple of fiction pieces and some spines with no wording on them at all.

There are CDs of music from the nineties and early two thousands. He and Blaire should probably talk because I don't recognize any of the titles, although I'm willing to bet she would.

And there, beneath a slew of papers and a sweatband, a slender volume with gold lines across the spine and no title.

I pull it out and flip to the center of the book, a well-worn place it seems as the pages fall open naturally.

There in the darkness where I find the sun and letters spun of gold.

For all the world to know yet I know none, fingers falling cold...

This isn't a biography, and it's not a spell. So what is it? My heart skips a beat as I flip through several other pages. The entire book is filled with poetry in a careful bold script. Captivated, I flip hurriedly through the first several chapters until Theo comes back, fresh and changed.

He clears his throat and I glance up from my seat at the end of his bed, the book in hand.

"You found my favorite book in the whole room," he comments offhandedly. "I don't mind you prying. Do you like it?"

The beauty between the cover of this book erases any discomfort at being caught snooping through his stuff. "I love poetry much more than normal fiction," I tell him. "The ones in here I've never read before, though. They seem to have a sense of depth and feeling. Not just empty words. You know?" I tap the page. "These are amazing."

He stares at me for a long moment. "That's what I felt, too, when I wrote them. It means a lot that you like them."

I shake my head. "I don't understand."

"My poetry. When things feel rough and it's not acceptable to let any of what I feel out...I find an outlet, Yas." He gestures to the book with his nose. "That's my poetry."

How can this guy, this powerful popular guy on campus who plays basketball and makes friends as easily as snapping his fingers, be a poet as well? It rocks my view of him in a way I'm not altogether comfortable with; how are the pieces of him ever going to line up?

"I love words." Theo takes a seat next to me, close enough for our thighs to rub together. "I find comfort in them. It's not really acceptable in my family, you know?

They look down on anything creative like this. If my dad found out about the poems he'd be pissed."

There's raw emotion in his admittance. For me, although I'm not sure I'm ready to admit it, knowing we have something in common makes things a bit lighter between us.

"I used to spend a lot of time in a library." I huff out a laugh. "Like, a *lot* of time. Words are pretty much my life." I stare sideways at him. "Reading your work means a lot to me."

"It means a lot that you'd tell me the truth, whether you like them or not." He tilts his head. "Somehow I think you always will."

Uh oh. "Well." I clear my throat. "I think they're lovely. You have talent whether your family wants to admit it or not. But I came here to pick you up so we can go study."

I don't want to stay in his room too long. Not where we're alone and I'm not sure I'll be able to keep this mask of apathy and distance.

"I'd rather not go to the library, actually," Theo admits. He gently pries the poetry book from me. "If you want to improve your reputation on campus, then we need to head to The Shed to start. We can study afterward."

It sounds like a make-out spot and I shiver. He notices.

"It's just the local hangout where students go to be seen. To spend time together," he clarifies, before he takes the book out of my hands. Then he looks at me, really looks at me, and stops. "Holy shit. You did something different with your hair. With your face. Are you wearing makeup?"

I fluff it out a bit to keep from being stiff and uncomfortable. "Just a little bit. Blaire decided I needed an overhaul. Surprise. You like it?"

"You look nice," he agrees. "But you always do. You don't actually need makeup. As long as you're confident and happy, I think it's great." He pushes away from the spot beside me and sets me with a look. "Can I take your books?"

I'd let my bag drop when I found the book of poetry. "You want to carry my books?" I ask.

"Of course. Why wouldn't I? It's just the right thing to do."

This seems more like a fantasy land. Maybe I'd never woken up from my good dreams.

Theo is really getting into this charade.

"Are you sure we're going to get to study?" I worry my fingers. "You said you wanted to get started tonight. You carrying my books, taking me to The Shed—"

"And we will," he assures me as he turns and grabs his jacket and a notebook. "We're just getting started for the night. This is building the foundation for us."

Us.

He reaches down to grab my bag, shouldering it and opening the door for me with his opposite hand.

The lump is back in my throat and I have a feeling it's not going anywhere.

"It's showtime," I mutter under my breath.

Theo hears me anyway. "Don't you worry. You're going to be perfect."

The door closes behind us. *Perfect*—yeah okay. The word has me remembering every single instance I've ever messed up in my life. Every piece of my mother's guidance where I thought I'd followed her instructions to the letter and somehow screwed things up regardless.

I'm so far from perfect it's not even funny.

Has Theo ever accidentally changed a living thing into a rock? Because yeah, I have. It took me all day to change that rock back into a mouse, and Gus still brings it up when he's irritated with me. Or how about when I mixed the wrong ingredients and turned our apartments into a sewer? The smell took weeks to get rid of.

Practice, Yasmine. It's Mom's voice in my head. *You have to practice or you're never going to get better. You'll squander your gifts.*

Theo doesn't seem to mind that I'm lost in my thoughts, and with my bag bumping his hip and keeping the distance between us, it feels safer. He's not pressuring me into conversation as he leads the way toward The Shed.

I appreciate it more than I'm willing to tell him.

He's stayed in his part of this. He's done everything he's promised to do, and delivered a smooth performance. I've got to silence my inner critic and participate in this if we want it to work. To sell it, as Theo said.

He's my saving grace in this case. It's time for me to step up and be that for him as well.

CHAPTER
SIXTEEN

"So."

Theo's voice startles me out of quiet contemplation and I jump, turning on him. "So, what?" I ask, my voice shaky.

"We might as well get to know each other a little better. As your boyfriend, there are certain things I'd know about you which I definitely don't at this point." His gaze turns questioning. "Do you want me to start or would you rather?"

Here I am acting like a nervous and shaking mouse. Rather than give into the undulating sensation in my stomach, a combination of excitement and worry, I channel Blaire. I channel Remi.

"There really isn't much to my story," I say. "I'm sure your life is much more interesting than mine. I was homeschooled and grew up in a library."

There. That sets the stage without revealing too much about me. It will at least show him why I'm so good in class, why I'm much better with books than with people.

"You go," I finish hastily.

"Well." Theo draws out the word, facing ahead. "I didn't want to come to this school. Nepotism at its finest, and not really a choice for me. I'm the oldest of four with three sisters. My father places a lot of expectations on me."

"What's it like to have such a big family? I only have one sister and she's older than I am."

"It's a lot to take in some days. There's always bickering, when Dad isn't around. Lots of joking around and horseplay but love, too," Theo admits. "Being the oldest comes with a lot of responsibility."

"You know, I never had a witch cotillion," I tell him, then instantly regret it. What is wrong with me? Talk about word vomit. Horrified, I hurry to recover. "I-I mean, my mother didn't believe in dancing. So there were never impromptu dance parties or anything like that. Gotta keep quiet in a library."

Theo stops dead in his tracks. "We're going to have to fix that."

I huff out a chuckle. "What? You're going to throw me a cotillion?"

"Nothing so extravagant, but one of those dance parties you're talking about? Entirely doable. I'm a pretty great dancer."

"I'm sure you're great at everything," I reply.

He shakes his head. "Definitely not everything. Especially if you talk to my parents. They'll tell you how things that are supposed to come easily for a guy like me have always been a bit of a struggle instead."

I like getting to know him. I also have a hard time believing there are things that Theo is not good at doing. Then again, he's the one who needs a tutor. And I liked the sound of dancing with him.

"We're going to have to test your moves and see if you can back up such a bold claim," I tease.

We stop in front of the door to what looks like a gardener's shed just to the right of the greenhouse where the school grows herbs and flowers for potions.

No one is around yet, it's just the two of us.

His smile remains reassuring as he pushes open the front door to the life and noise inside the space.

He leads the way inside where TVs are playing, silently, casting bright images against the walls. Pop music plays instead of the noise from the shows. Surprising, I think as I look around. We're adjacent to the student campus parking and a good walk away from the main buildings but the inside is a mixture of 1950s diner and a modern-day Waffle House.

Which I only know because Blaire showed me one when we went out the first time.

Some kind of spell cast on The Shed makes the interior much more spacious than you'd guess from the outside. There are booths along both walls and the middle of the floor is a black-and-white checkered tile. Definitely embracing the fifties-diner vibe. I imagine people strolling between the booths with a pad and a pencil ready to take orders, or a short-tempered chef slapping burger patties down on a sizzling grill.

It's an experience, and nothing like anything I've seen before.

Theo jerks his chin and we take a seat in one of the booths, both on the same side. My heart clutches as he slides closer and closer and I'm stuck between the wall and him.

It's not a bad place for me to be.

My imaginary scenario with a server isn't far off, either. A waitress walks over and although she doesn't have a pad and a pencil, she asks for our order.

"We'll just take a plate of mozzarella sticks and some fries, please. Two cokes." Theo orders for both of us.

"Sounds great," I manage.

When we're alone again, I pull out my notes on spellcasting from the bag Theo dropped on the opposite side of the booth.

It's so much easier to focus on him and what he needs rather than myself. It's the way I've been trained my entire life. I'm the one with the power, with the knowledge, to serve my people. To join the caste of Clerics and give back to the community. It's my only purpose.

"You've got an exam coming up and I think that's where we need to focus," I say.

Theo looks less than enthused. I hardly blame him. Exams aren't my happy place either.

"Before you get into the actual spell casting portion, you need to start with the basics, learn them intimately, and go from there."

"I'm moderately familiar with the basics. I guess I stumble somewhere between knowing and executing," he says, pausing to offer one of those heart stopping grins to the waitress as she delivers the two cokes for us.

She's an older student with her hair twisted in an easy bun and she looks as flustered as anyone at the potency of his smile.

"It's symbols. Sigils. The intentions behind the magic. All of those things are going to be integral toward the execution portion of it," I say. "It might take a few days for you to get the hang of this but I know you can do it. At least it's the weekend."

"Yeah. You know, I always think Sunday is a sad day. But the day before is a Sat-urday."

Despite how horrible it is, I chuckle, a genuine laugh.

"And here I wasn't sure I'd get to see that smile of yours," he replies in a low tone.

Uh oh. My breath catches and I bite down on my lip.

"You…you shouldn't say those things."

"Why not?" He wants to know. "You're my girlfriend. Aren't you?"

"I've never been anyone's girlfriend," I say. "This is going to take me some time to get used to, Theo."

"I know. But it's okay."

I chuckle and say, "How do you think this is anywhere near okay?"

"Because I'm a fighter. And you've agreed to help me, so now I'm going to do everything in my power to fight for you."

The moment shatters when the server returns with our fried food. And I'm thankful she did because I'm not ready to hear what Theo really thinks about me being perpetually single for twenty-one years.

The door to The Shed opens and in walks a group of people I instantly recognize. Theo's clique, the one he hangs out with on a regular basis. Crap. They're going to know immediately that this is a sham, whatever is happening between us. They know him better than anyone else.

He might be confident in his acting skills, but he severely overestimates mine.

The group of three beeline straight toward us. I'm pretty sure their names are James, Piper, and something with a B. Betsy? Becky? Whatever it is, the determination on her face has me nearly forgetting my own name until Theo turns to me.

"Don't worry. I got this."

He's asking me without saying the words to trust him and I want to. I desperately want to believe he has this handled. He sees the fear in my eyes and nods before he swivels around to face his friends, his arm thrusting easily behind my neck in a possessive gesture.

"Hey guys." His voice is as smooth as glass. "What's up?"

"Theo," James replies.

The three of them slide into the opposite side of the booth and Piper pushes my bag onto the floor.

"Gang, this is Yasmine." He tightens his hold on my shoulder and jerks me closer to him so that I'm underneath the safety of his arm. "Yas, you know Piper, Becky, and James?"

The arm around me is for good measure and I

know it without having to look at Theo. Just like I know the others are putting on happy faces for his benefit and not because they're delighted to officially meet me.

We've all seen each other before.

We have classes together and although they appear friendly and open to me joining the inner circle, this is nothing but pretend.

"It's great to actually meet you," James begins. "You came into the semester late, right? But you always raise your hand in class."

Oh, sure. He laughed right along with Kim and Courtney that first day.

He stares at me like I'm the one with all the answers and he's not sure where I actually fit, since I'm with Theo now. These people operate on levels, or inside of boxes. Something that allows them to place people in what they think are accurate categories and act accordingly from there.

I've stepped outside of where I belong by being with Theo.

"It's good to meet you, too. I'm catching up slowly but hopefully coming in late won't make much of a difference in the long run," I say carefully.

I grab my straw and stick in my mouth, to keep from having to talk to them, and notice my fingers trembling. It's not like me to be this nervous. I'm used to talking to new people at the library all the time.

Except these are Theo's friends and I've accepted their lines in the sand whether I want to or not.

"Yasmine, how did the two of you meet?" Piper asks.

"It seems like only yesterday he was out with Helena and now here you are."

Her voice is friendly, perky, and spears right through me.

"Yas is in a couple of my classes and we hit it off," Theo interjects smoothly. He takes the lead in the conversation without any effort. "Things naturally progressed between us."

It should be an open and shut thing. Yet life rarely follows the path you wish it to take.

"So this is official? It's not because Helena called it off?" Becky asks. "I mean, you don't have to go from hot girl to *her*."

And by *her* she means me.

I expected a bit of venom. Of course, it's bound to happen. Yet it seems as though some girls feel a certain way about Theo claiming me as his and it's not a good way.

I push against him to get out of the booth and the suffocating presence of his friends. "Maybe this is a conversation I shouldn't be a part of," I say. "I can go."

Theo refuses to budge. He sits, blocking my way, as solid as stone. "No, I want you here." His voice gives nothing away and neither does his expression. Both are cool without being hostile or outright pissed in any way. He's not trembling the way I am.

"Oh?" Piper questions.

"What I do and with whom is none of your business. She's mine, Piper, and it has nothing to do with Helena or anyone else."

Becky shrugs. "It just seems to me the timing is a little suspect. You know?"

James looks curious, but also like he'd rather be anywhere else.

Finally Theo stands, digging deep in his pocket and pulling out money before tossing it on the table. He holds out his hand to me and after struggling to remove my bag from underneath the table, I take the outstretched palm.

"Are you ready to go?" he asks as he pulls me to my feet.

I nod.

"Then let's get out."

Linking our fingers together, electricity zaps between us and he tugs me toward the door, away from the three vultures trying to pick me, pick us, apart.

CHAPTER
SEVENTEEN

We leave the café without a backward glance, Theo hurrying us along. Rather than heading back to his dorm or someplace quiet to actually study, he turns, heading toward the campus student parking lot.

"Here." He stops in front of a motorcycle and after grabbing an extra helmet from a case on the back of the seat, he tosses it to me. "Hop on," he says. "Let's get out for a while. There's actually some place I wanted to go instead of The Shed."

"I thought you wanted to be seen."

"Yeah, and we were. Now it's time to go."

I stare at the sleek lines of the black bike, the two wheels and the gleaming handlebars. Of course Theo would ride a motorcycle. It fits his image perfectly. And seeing it up close and personal does nothing to extinguish the sliver of fear worming its way down my spine.

"I've never been on a bike before." My voice still trembles.

"You can trust me, Yasmine." He reaches over and lifts my chin up to meet his gaze. "I won't let anything happen to you. I've handled this bike well enough to know what to expect with a passenger."

I want to believe him.

I want to give him all my trust and place my safety in his capable hands. To lean on someone who will have my back in a way no one else has before, not even the people I thought would always be there.

Yet—

My hands are back to tingling although there's no weird shadows right now. I don't want to act crazy in front of Theo.

"Let me take this." He gently pries my bag from over my shoulder and places it into the empty satchel where he'd grabbed the helmets.

Theo is the first to straddle the bike and leaves enough room on the seat for me to slide behind him. I wrap my arms around him, grateful the helmet hides my expression. I want to sigh as I mold myself to the muscled planes of his back.

Okay, this isn't so bad.

He starts the ignition and throttles the bike, the engine roaring to life in the near silent night. Then, Theo maneuvers the bike out of the parking spot and off campus.

His body is warm. Am I tingling this time because of him because of his nearness, or the motor's vibrations?

It's a dream come true. I'm riding off into the sunset

with the most popular guy on campus. The handsome somebody chose me. Do dreams really come true or is this a plateau before everything drops off into my usual bad luck?

I lean closer. The night air shivers along the exposed skin on my arms as we leave campus behind.

I'm not sure how long we're on the road before Theo pulls into another parking lot. At the opposite end of the lot rises a towering Italian renaissance villa surrounded by lush gardens. Spotlights illuminate the great facade of the place and turn the columns into glowing pillars.

My ears ring in the sudden quiet when he cuts off the engine.

"This is fabulous," I mutter.

"It's my favorite place to come," Theo tells me. He makes sure the kickstand is in place before he swings his leg over the bike and helps me do the same. I'm a little wobbly.

"I can see why you like it. Where are we?" I ask.

"The house is now a local art museum. The gardens surrounding the place, like twenty acres, are all private. Sometimes the museum gives out tickets to the gardens but not often."

"Wait, I don't understand. How are the gardens private but the museum is open to the public?" The light of the setting sun casts deep shadows along the green foliage.

Excitement buzzes in my veins. I've never been to an art museum before. Tonight has a whole lot of firsts for me and somehow, the wonder of the gardens and the entire aura of the place eclipses even the excitement of riding a motorcycle.

Theo tucks his helmet over one of the handlebars and holds out his hands for mine. Of course I get stuck, and by the time I manage to peel the helmet off, my ear is trapped by the straps. He has to gently help pry me free.

"It's a little complicated. Until my family moved completely into the magical world, these lands used to belong to us. I lived in the house growing up. The lands went into a historic trust along with the building, so they aren't really private, but most museum patrons have to purchase a completely separate ticket to the gardens. The money goes toward the upkeep and my mom and dad like to pretend we still own the gardens."

He turns to face the opening to the gardens, an arbor covered in pink and yellow honeysuckle. "I like to come here after the museum closes and…pretend like it's still mine, too. How do you feel about a walk?"

"I think it's a great idea."

I slide my arm through his offered elbow and Theo guides me through the arbor and into the waiting gardens. The evening air is soaked with the scent of the blooms even this late into the season, holding a hint of the cold weather to come. The beauty of the beds takes my breath away. Towering trees would offer shade in the summer with their branches filled with leaves and swaying overhead.

I can imagine a blanket beneath one of them, spread out on the soft moss with an open book in my hand.

My mind flashes back to the strange grimoire and I forcefully shut those thoughts down.

The beauty of the gardens. That's what I need to focus on. The warmth of the boy guiding me along lazy trails of cobblestone and mulch until we stop in front of a thick-trunked red maple, its leaves shifting into the colors of autumn.

"My dad carved our family initials into this tree," Theo tells me. "When I was little and my sisters were still toddling around in diapers. It meant a lot to see a piece of us here, like it would stay forever. You know?"

I glance up at him, surprised. "It's really nice how willing you are to talk about this," I reply. "About your home and your past. Do you miss the house?"

He leads us over to a curving stone bench seated directly across from the maple tree and the stones set just so beneath it. The arrangement takes the natural scene into more of an art piece than anything else. In the dim light I can't see where Theo's dad made his carving, his mark on this place.

"I only miss the gardens," Theo admits. He leans his elbows on his knees and stares at the tree. "I discovered my magic out here."

"Really? How did it happen?" I'm asking too many questions and not giving much in return.

Theo doesn't seem to mind. He looks lost to his memories, to the draw of this place and whatever magic he discovered on that day. "I was out here by myself and I ran too fast along the paths. I tripped, landed in a rosebush. Found I had the ability to heal my cuts with a thought while screaming about the pain."

I like imagining him in this place. It's so different from campus, and it seems fitting that I'm seeing a different side of Theo than anything he's shown me before. I want to tell him about how I always knew I had magic. How my powers were fostered from a young age and were guided to grow in a certain direction.

None of those things come out.

"I have another reason for bringing you here, though," he admits. He snaps his fingers and from beneath the tree a red-and-white checked picnic blanket unfurls out of nowhere. "I thought it would be great to watch the sunset on our first official date. You did really well back there, handling those guys. Now we can have our dessert."

My mouth is dry again and my stomach achingly hollow despite my heart filling to bursting.

I want to remember this moment of him being here, seeing me, surrounded by the beauty. It's all pretend, but right now it sure doesn't feel like it.

"Come on." He takes my hand and leads me to the waiting blanket.

Folding my body down, I sit across from him, not realizing that from the slight uphill position we have a nearly perfect view of the sunset on the horizon, painting the sky a myriad of gorgeous peaches and purples.

The other shoe is bound to drop sooner than later. Tonight is too great, too perfect.

"You really planned all this?" I squint at him. "Seems like a gimmick to me."

"Not a gimmick," he insists quietly. "Maybe I feel like

I found someone in this entire place who actually meets me on my level. Someone who will understand when I talk about art and books and sunsets, without giving me shit or mocking me."

I blanche. "People mock you?"

He shakes his head and a lock of hair falls over his face. "I don't give them the chance because I don't talk to them about the real me. They see what they want to see and I encourage it."

"You trust me enough to show me the real you." How? He's never spoken to me before.

"I saw an opening to talk to you, and I took it." There's the mischief. "Do you blame me?"

"We're not going to get our studying done," I murmur.

"We have time," he insists, holding out a strawberry for me to take. "We have time, Yas. Why don't you tell me more about you?"

"What do you want to know?" I ask.

"Let's start with how you've made it this far without ever riding a motorcycle, or going on a date."

I focus on the parts of me that have no ties to what happened to the library and tell Theo about my favorite foods, the stories I've read. I tell him about my sister and how she likes to sneak around with her boyfriend. All the while, I wait for something about the moment to crack and show me the harsh, cold reality underneath.

Instead, Theo stays a complete gentleman. We talk about everything and nothing, his stupid jokes making me laugh time and again.

Right before we leave, he packs up the picnic and

walks me past a fountain. The gently bubbling water is a balm to the soul.

"I had fun today, you know," he says. "Do you want to make a wish? I've got a couple of coins on me. I think I can manage a wish for both of us."

"What can I possibly wish for?" I ask with a laugh.

"Whatever you want." He digs a coin out of his pocket and holds it out to me.

I flip the piece of silver between my fingers, the metal catching the last hints of light. Lights have begun to glow along the path. Whatever I want…it seems like a stretch. Nothing in my life so far has been about what I want, and being here with him is a dream come to life. Which leaves me doubting everything.

I wish…

Closing my eyes, I form the wish in my head. The coin practically leaps from my hands and plunks into the fountain. When it disappears underneath the water, a weight lifts off my chest. Despite everything, for the first time in years, I find myself excited, not afraid.

"Good job."

Theo takes me in his arms, grabbing me around the waist and pulling me toward him. "Do you want to know what *I* wished for?"

"I don't know if I'm strong enough to hear it. Or strong enough to hope it will come true if you tell me," I whisper.

"Let me show you."

No, I'm not afraid of anything, not even when Theo lowers his mouth to my lips and kisses a corner. Then the other. He's patient and gentle while he judges my reaction, his hands just as soft on my spine. They trail down to my hips, up to my ribs, then settle once again around my waist as he waits for me to be sure.

I'm beyond sure.

I lift my hands to frame his face and smile, just before he dips down to kiss me for real.

I open for him and every part of my body and my magic sings at the contact. How strong he feels to touch and the first small groan when I dart my tongue out to tangle with his own.

He takes the kiss deeper at my small request and his hips grind against mine until heat scorches through me.

Making my body his.

His touch has me panting, wanting, trembling. How can I not when Theo has my name on his lips like a prayer? He touches me and tastes me and his skin is sun-warmed silk over stone. I want more. I want the kiss to last forever.

Pretend just went out of the window.

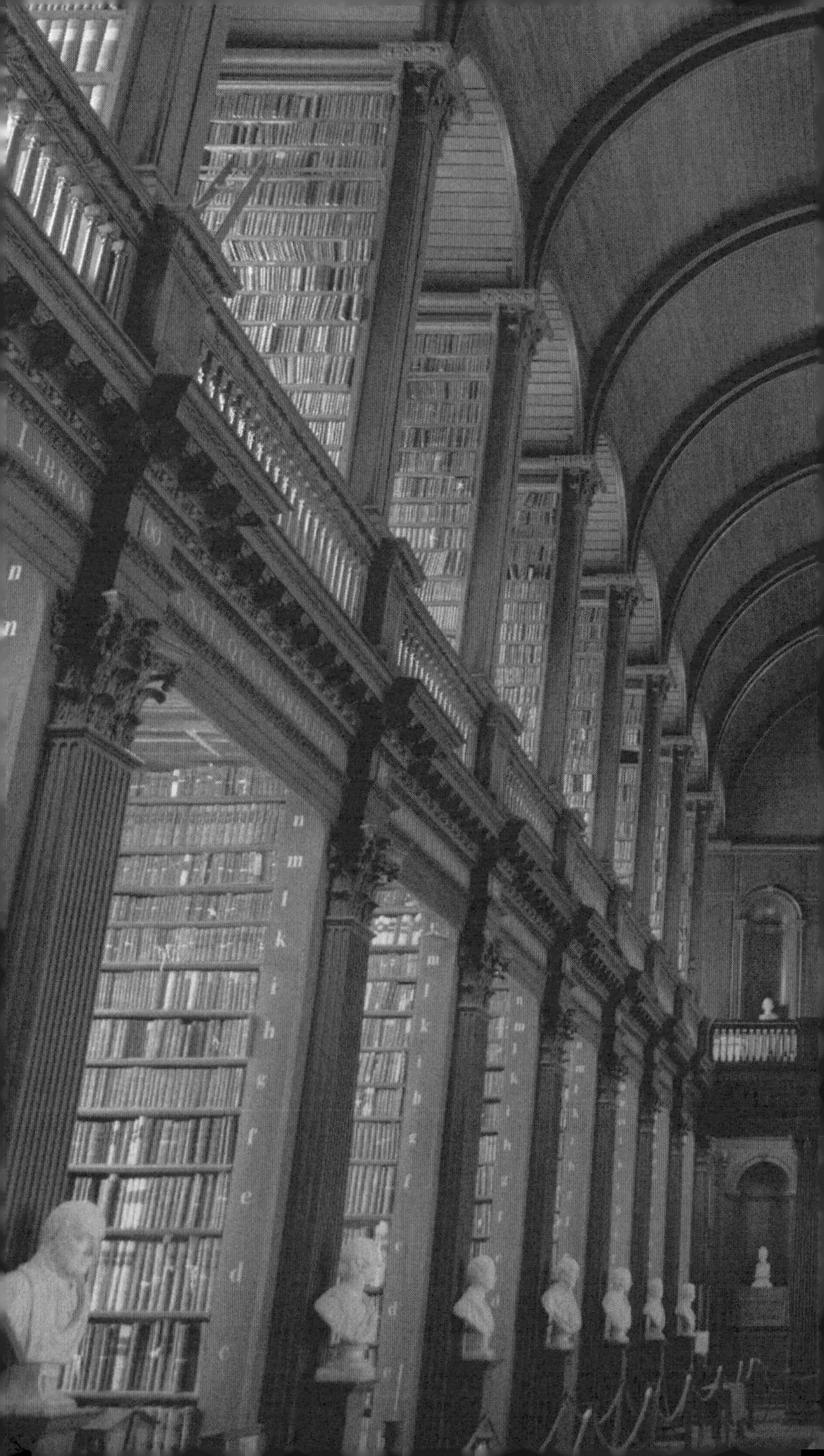

CHAPTER
EIGHTEEN

The kiss leaves me reeling and forgetting my own name.

It comes back to me in small pieces once Theo takes a step in the opposite direction but the breathing room isn't enough to get me back to center. Not when I'm off in the clouds with my lips tingling and the rest of me on fire. His fingers linger on my cheek, his eyes dark and serious and vulnerable.

Whatever he sees on my face, he smiles.

The smile undoes the last of my reservation.

This isn't pretend.

For some reason, some unfathomable reason, Theo *does* like me. He likes me enough to throw me a sunset picnic, and kiss me, and ask about my day. To actually care about the answer. I get the feeling he wished for me the same way I wished for him.

It's impossible. It's magic.

I ride a wave of exhilaration all the way back to campus. Theo walks me to my dorm and I cling to him.

Neither one of us seems to mind and I'm not chasing shadows this time.

I'm floating and falling at the same time. I've never felt this way and part of me wonders if this is infatuation or if this is the end, and I'll never feel this about anyone else again.

Some people meet their mates in school. Why can't I be one of them?

It's too early to say, and questioning it takes away from the value of now.

We stop at the entrance of X House and Theo stares at the doorway, the windows. The general air of neglect about the place. "You know, I've never actually been inside," he mutters. "It's kind of an unspoken no-no among the guys in my dorm."

"Is that your way of trying to get an invitation out of me?" Because there's time, as he says.

"Not tonight, but yes. Eventually I'm going to expect an invitation." His voice drops low, softer, and it takes everything inside of me not to rise up on the tips of my toes and claim another kiss from him.

"I'll see you tomorrow for breakfast, if you're up for it," he says.

"Breakfast is good, but we do have that test coming up. And you still have to study for it. Since no real studying was done tonight, I feel a little bit guilty." Not really. Only a tiny piece of guilt in the grand scheme of things.

Theo lets out a bark of laughter. "We'll get to studying soon because you're right, I really do need to be better prepared for this test. We're still going to have breakfast together, though."

"Yes," I agree without any hesitation. "We will."

This is like being in one of my romance novels, I think as I make my way inside my room. The door shuts behind me and I collapse against the wood with a happy sigh.

I lift a hand to my heart and rub there. These feelings are so strong, so warm. And I—

My joy is interrupted by a familiar voice calling out, "I've been waiting for you to come back. You certainly took your time!"

My eyes pop open. Remi is there, sitting on my bed with her hands on her lap and a giant smile on her face. My sister is here. How?

"Oh my gosh!" With a running start I launch myself at her and tackle her, both of us laughing.

Remi is in my room, and has been waiting there for me, with Blaire.

Remi wraps her arms around me, squeezing me tightly. "Man, I'm glad that you're happy, sis," she says, "because you have a hell of a mess to fix. You have no idea what kind of chaos you left behind!"

I don't want to think about messes because my sister is here and I missed her.

"Do you know how long I've been waiting for you?" she asks.

"Not nearly as long as I've been waiting for you." I pull back to examine her. She's flawless, as usual. There is no hint of a scar or shadow to mark her ordeal at the library. "You're okay. You weren't caught in the fire?"

She nods. "Yeah, I'm fine. I'm fine." She does a double check of me, too, worry lines fanning out from her eyes. "Are you?"

"I've been keeping your sister entertained with stories of my fabulous upbringing," Blaire says, jokingly flipping her hair over her shoulder. "It turns out we have a mutual love for several bands. Which automatically makes Remi pretty awesome, in my opinion."

"She's definitely awesome. Are you sure you're okay? *How* are you okay? You were—" I don't want Blaire to know the details about the library fire.

Remi answers with, "We're okay. I'm sorry you worried. I know Mom probably didn't tell you the truth of what happened. How could she?"

"What do you mean, we?"

"Me and Atlas barely escaped the library before the fire. I think that something about my blood must be keeping me safe. We got out just in time." Her lips purse. "I went to meet him because I couldn't stand to watch those fuckers at your ascension ceremony fawn over you like you were a toy for them."

I glance over at Blaire but she shrugs. "Remi told me a little bit about what happened. Don't worry," she says. "I'm not going to say a word. Everything we say in this room stays between us."

"Blaire..." I send her a pleading look. If Remi's here, then it isn't for a social visit. The gravity of the situation crashes down on me and the tingling is back in my hands with a vengeance.

Is this the other shoe? Potentially. And it has nothing

to do with Theo and everything to do with the past I've been forced to outrun.

"You have to swear," I add. "This is serious."

She crosses her fingers in the shape of an X over her lips. "Trust me, girl, I've got you. Both of you. You can say anything you need to say in front of me. Or I can leave and give you privacy, totally fine.."

She looks like she'd rather have all of her teeth pulled than leave the room now. It's a lot to think about, and I weigh the options before sighing. "It's fine. You can stay."

I shoot her a final warning glance before I untangle myself from Remi.

"I'm happy to see you, and I missed you. But why are you here?" I ask my sister. "And what do you mean, I left behind a mess? You know they forced me out, right?"

Her smile melts away inch by inch until she's stone faced, her eyes boring into mine. "You weren't forced. Eli said…you wanted some space while they investigated."

"Lies," I hiss out between my suddenly clenched teeth.

"Things haven't been the same without you, Yas. Let's just say that. It's like something dark has fallen over the coven since your failed ascension. The fire at the library was just the beginning," she says. "I don't trust anyone. They're acting really strange."

"What do you mean, darkness? What kind of darkness?" It sounds like it's straight out of a book, and I don't trust Remi not to over exaggerate.

She groans, flopping back on the bed and stealing my pillow for her own.

"You know they don't talk to me because I'm human, but I know things. I listen and they pay no attention because, hey, pathetic little mortal. Which is how I know the coven leaders aren't acting like themselves."

"Not if they're lying and telling you I left. I couldn't get here on my own, Remi," I insist. "Mom brought me here. They kicked me out."

"They're spouting off all kinds of new rules like they're the heads of some kind of military operation. It's almost like they're possessed, and not by Casper the friendly ghost, if you know what I mean. It's a dark force. A lot's happened. The town was evacuated. Lark and Eli are unfocused, walking all jerky like puppets on a string..." Remi trails off. "I had to find you, get you to come back and see for yourself."

I thought back to the odd way the coven witches moved during my birthday. How they were wading through the mist, not acting correctly, then it seemed like they came out of a thrall. What if they never had?

What if something was still going on and they sent me away not for fear of what I'd do, but because of what *they* would do?

"Is Mom a part of this?" I ask.

Remi shakes her head. "Mom is mom. You know how she is; she's already a dark force of nature. It's not like that's going to change anytime soon."

It's not an answer and worry begins to gnaw at me, causing an empty hole in my gut previously filled with strawberries, wishes, and kisses.

"Are they just acting differently or are they doing weird things?" It makes a difference. It makes a lot of difference, considering I'd seen what happened at the failed ceremony and Remi had not.

"Lark barely comes out of her rooms anymore, and Eli has taken to holding secret ceremonies. He won't tell Mom about them, but she knows he's been calling the other members into the woods and they don't come out for hours. When they do, they won't speak to anyone," Remi replies. She strokes a finger down Gus's back once he comes out to say hello. "It's really weird, Yas. I get a creepy feeling on the back of my neck whenever I'm around them and it's starting to freak me out. The shadows seem darker, like they move on their own. I know I'm human but…it's there. It's noticeable."

It makes sense. I hate that it makes sense because I saw the same thing the other day. Whatever presence I felt here is an extension of what's taking up residence at home.

What's pulling the strings of the coven like a deranged puppet master?

"You not getting initiated to the caste of Clerics is a bigger deal than we thought, Yas," Remi finishes. "Things are changing, and not in a good way. Like it's all connected."

I wince at the casual way Remi gives up one of my biggest secrets. The Clerics.

I hadn't brought it up to Blaire before, after what Amy told me on my first day here. Now, I slowly turn to face her, to take in her reaction.

And there sits Blaire in her seat, all fluffy pink hair

and absolute shock. It's a wonder she's managing to keep a straight face.

"Surprise?" I offer weakly.

"I can't tell anyone about you being from a line of Clerics," she hisses. "Are you kidding me right now, Yazzy?"

"Not kidding you," Remi answers for me.

"The Clerics…are nothing but bad news. Everyone thought the last one had been burned at the stake. Now here you are—" Blaire breaks off, shaking her head. "Forget your reputation. They'll take up pitchforks!"

"I don't understand what's so bad about being from a line of Clerics. Just because the last known Cleric was a bad dude doesn't mean we all are." My mom certainly isn't bad, just strict.

"Do you know what kind of shit went down the last time there were any Clerics out there? Like, seriously?" Blaire goes pale faced and leans down with her elbows on her knees, gasping for air and trying not to let us notice.

Remi and I share a look.

"We've grown up with our Mom as a Cleric," she says to Blaire. "We only know the stories she told us."

"Well, in olden times, covens were ruled by high priests and priestesses but only those from the Clerics could commune with the divine. They were a step above the usual rules. People started to say anyone who ascended to the Cleric in their coven was touched by the mother."

I've heard about her. The divine mother, Kaelyah, also called the good mother.

"It's said the divine mother reached down to her covens, her protected ones, and told them of a dream she had where she would be betrayed. Apparently she called up her allies and sought to protect the covens. But the Cleric in the coven who had been so blessed by her... he also had the dream. He saw the power of the mother and a way for him to have it for his own."

I shiver even though the temperature in the room hasn't changed. Without having heard it before, I knew where the story would go.

"The Cleric betrayed his coven, all covens, and burned the other Clerics who had less power than him. He seized it for his own," Blaire continues.

This isn't anywhere near to the story I'd been told growing up. Nothing close.

Talk about a history lesson. Beside me, Remi is just as shellshocked as I am.

"The divine mother, the high priests, and the high priestesses all joined together to fight back against the rogue Cleric. The power he'd stolen had corrupted him and turned him into something dark and unnatural." Blaire pauses for effect even though it's not necessary. She's going green around the gills too, and the blood drains from my face because I know what she's going to say. "He changed into a horned god. There was no going back from that."

Shit.

"They say the good mother trapped him inside a book and he is to remain there until the blood of another Cleric sets him free. Which is why no one is upset that Clerics have died out. The last known Cleric was burned at the stake even though he'd had his power stolen from him, as a safeguard. Only they haven't disappeared. Have they?" Blaire's laugh is high pitched and a little frenzied. "Because here you are. And you haven't bled on any books lately, Yazzy, have you?"

My laugh sounds just as crazed as hers. "Of course not. I'm a librarian. It's not like I make a habit of slicing open a vein."

"What happens if he's set free?" Remi asks. Her dark eyes are unreadable.

"According to the stories, and who's to say if these are real or not, but he's sworn vengeance on the world of magic. And only the one who sets him free can return him to his prison," Blaire answers.

Me. It's me. It can't be real, except it is, and the spotlight is on my shoulders. I set him free through some strange manipulation of fate and he's been hunting me since, to take me down before I can put him back in a book.

Like I'd even know where to start.

"It doesn't make sense, though," Blaire continues. "If all of the Clerics were killed then how... how is it possible that you are one? That you were groomed to be the *one*?"

"I actually don't know how to answer you," I mutter. Lightheaded and a little dizzy, I rub circles along my stomach. It doesn't help.

"I know."

Blaire and I turn to look at Remi in unison. "So you've heard this story before?" I ask shakily. And apparently hid it from me.

What else does my sister know? What other secrets has she kept locked away because she doesn't trust me?

Or for my own good?

"The divine mother hid one lone survivor," Remi says, not bothering to look ashamed. "And passed down the information on their whereabouts from her child, and so on. Mother to child. Since that time, only one Williams's daughter has possessed the knowledge and the gift. From Grandma to Mom, and from Mom…to you, Yasmine."

Damn it, it's me. Now I get what Mom meant as far as my magic, that of childhood being replaced by something greater. Uniting me with the kind of magic used to create the Horned God.

I'm going to be sick.

I want to tear through the room and destroy everything in my path, to make the outside space look the way I feel on the inside. To tear through the boy-band posters on the wall and whip everything into a frenzy like it will somehow get rid of this distraught feeling gnawing at my bones.

My fate is tied to the Horned God.

With even more on my plate than just my reputation at the academy and my fake relationship with Theo Acaster, I have to try to get rid of this ticking time bomb before it explodes right in my face.

"What am I going to do?" I stare at the floor and surge to my feet, my stomach dropping with the movement. "I can't stay like this. I've got to do something to make it all go away."

"Hey, whatever you need, I'm here. I am up to help in whatever way I can."

"It's a great offer, Blaire, but you should stay as far away from this as possible. Is Mom safe, at least?" I turn to Remi.

"The coven members are all acting like puppets. The magical border has been shut down around the coven. That's what I didn't tell you before." She gnaws on her thumbnail, the way she always does when she's nervous. "Atlas and I were able to escape in time before the barrier closed, but Mom is still inside. That's why I came to the university to get some help. I'm not sure who else to ask, sis. I'm sorry."

It's my fault. The thought circles in my head, spiraling around and around without any end in sight. I'm the reason this is all happening and the coven is involved.

The Horned God is free and he's gathering the powers of the coven to make his return. He'll be gunning for me, to kill me, to make sure I don't stand in his way anymore.

Since I'm the only one who would be able to put him back.

I run my hands through my hair and pull, like the pain will somehow center me.

"We've wasted enough time on talking, though." Remi stands as well, keeping Gus cradled to her palm. He's been oddly silent this whole time but I can't look at him. Not when he knows the truth as well as I do. "You need to pack your bag. We have to return to the coven and deal with this."

"With what?" I ask.

"The big bad. Surely you've got the brains to do it. You're the smartest person I know, Yasmine. And maybe you can free Mom from whatever has her."

"The Horned God..." I breathe.

"He's got to want something more than just your mother, though," Blaire says. "What could he want?"

Their gazes both fall to me. "Have you been seeing his shadow?" Remi asks.

Slowly, I nod. "I did the other day." But then something strikes me. "Wait... How do you know about him?"

"I may be human, but I hear things. Mostly murmuring from Mom. Her worries." Her gaze hardens on me. "Damn it. He's been searching for you, then. Summoning you to return to him." Gus hops up to her shoulder as Remi grabs me by the arms. "I'm afraid of what will happen if you don't come home with me. Right now."

My heart leaps into my throat at the knock at the door. Loud, rapping. Ominous. The Horned God...is here?

CHAPTER NINETEEN

Dizzy, I'm about to pass out from the stress of wondering what the hell is going on when Atlas pushes through the door. Sweaty, shocked. There are dark circles under his eyes and his hair is a lion's mane around his head.

He glances at me and tries for a smile, failing miserably. "Remi told me everything on the drive," he admits.

Atlas closes the door behind him and leans hard on the wood, blocking the exit with his body. "I always thought your family was just into some weird cult shit, not that magic was real."

It's so easy to forget that he's human, too. Just like Remi.

"No one is going to turn me into a frog, will they?" He sounds worried.

What did I ever find attractive about Atlas? I wonder distantly as I stare at him right back. He's so *ordinary* next to Theo. Lacking a spark that takes him from cute to downright handsome.

"He's suffering from fear of the Brothers Grimm," Remi says as she moves to take his hand and draw him further into the room. Each step her boyfriend takes is hesitant. "Since all the witches he's heard about are from fairy tales. He's been stressed since we made it onto the campus. Do you know how long it took us to get here?"

She shrinks a little, as though the weight of her exhaustion has finally started to make itself known.

"You're going to be fine," I tell him. "No one will turn you into a toad. Witches aren't like that."

Except some of them are.

I wish I could call Theo and tell him what's going on. How all of this has gotten out of hand and I'm not even sure where to start. My head aches. Even if I know the ins and outs of casting spells, using those spells for combat is a foreign concept.

No reading is going to prepare me for going to war with an ancient and newly freed god. Not a real god, I correct myself, just a guy who managed to steal himself some god-like powers.

There's really no difference but it helps to think about him as a man instead.

Theo might not have the book smarts he needs to make it through his classes, but he knows about other things. He'd be so much better at keeping a cool head.

"Yasmine, I know what you're thinking," Blaire says to me.

"You have no idea," I mumble.

"Do you intend to pull Theo into this, too?"

Okay, so she knows exactly what I'm thinking, and I'm ashamed. One date at The Shed, one *fake* date, doesn't make him ready to be my knight in shining armor. It doesn't make him ready or willing to race into battle for me.

"If the Horned God is as powerful as Remi has let on, then we're going to need help," I say out loud. Like it somehow makes my desire to ask Theo better or justified.

"We don't really have time to gather reinforcements, sis," Remi says. She clings closer to Atlas. "We've got to go. Pack your bag. We're out of here."

What choice do I have?

Silently, ignoring Blaire's silent plea for me to look at her and talk this out, I grab my backpack. In goes the personal grimoire, a satchel of herbs I might need. My crystals and my magic starter kit. And there, already tucked into the depths of the fabric bag, my favorite comfort book. The highlander romance.

It's seen me through my worst times.

Good old Seamus who was willing to do anything it took to protect his love from harm. What would I do if the roles were reversed and I was in an actual committed relationship with Theo? Would I be strong enough to walk away?

Did I want to walk away? Or is it selfish to drag him into this?

My decision rings through me with terrible clarity. I at least want to let him know, to show this side of myself, and see what he says. To give him the choice whether it's selfish of me or not.

"I'm going to talk to Theo," I tell everyone out loud.

My sister squeaks, disgruntled. "We're wasting time! Who is Theo? We've got to *go*, Yas. The longer we take to get home, the greater the chance we're going to be too late to help Mom."

I'm a fighter. Theo said those words to me. *I'm going to do everything in my power to fight for you.*

Will he, though, once he realizes what's really going on?

This is more than he'd signed up for when he offered up a fake relationship. But there's no one else on campus I feel safe enough to confide in, and I can't do this alone. There's only me and my human sister.

"Take Gus," I tell Remi. "I'll be right behind you."

I'm going to need my familiar but I'm not risking taking him on a motorcycle with me. I'm too scared that something will happen to him.

"You can't be serious right now."

"I'm serious. You go and I'll meet you at the outskirts of the barrier."

"How do you even know where it is?" she asks. "Do you have any idea what a risk we even took to come here?"

"Trust me." It isn't a good idea for her to trust me but I have to do this. Call it an intuitive nudge. Call it stupidity. I need to talk to Theo. "I'll find the barrier and I'll meet you there. Okay? I won't be long."

After packing my magic supplies, I sneak out of the

dorm. It's way past curfew and if anyone sees me, there's no way for me to make it off campus.

The hastily muttered spell settles on my skin and slowly I lose sight of myself. The iridescence of the magic reflects the light from overhead, turning me invisible.

It's funny to think that the first time I went up to Theo's room had been only hours earlier. It seems like the path is familiar now and one I've done a thousand times before instead of just tonight.

The magic keeps me from being seen but not felt. I'm careful to skirt around several of the staff walking the paths through the campus as though on the alert for students out of bed past curfew.

It's only a matter of time before I stand in front of his door, just as conflicted as I felt when I first headed here. A large of part of me screams that it isn't right to drag Theo into this. His only sin is helping me, kissing me, trying to bolster my reputation.

I don't deserve him.

I've been lying to him by omission from the start.

Yet my hand lifts of its own accord and raps on the door.

Seconds later Theo answers, standing shirtless in front of me again. Does the man ever wear a shirt? It takes me a full five seconds to catch my breath and roll my tongue back into my mouth.

"It's me," I whisper. "Let me in? Please?"

Theo quirks a brow high. "And just how do I know that the invisible person whispering outside my room is Yasmine and not a ghoulish impostor?"

I reach out and flick him, lightly, on the nipple. Theo makes a good show of flinching, of showing none of his confusion, as he steps aside to let me in. The door shuts behind him and at once I think how absolutely lucky I am that we're alone in his dorm room.

Doing my best to ignore his body falls just short of the mark. He's ripped in all the right ways. And it's not just basketball practice that has given him the muscles of his chest and forearms. His torso looks as though I can run my fingers down his abs and play him like an instrument.

Damn.

This is the man who kissed me earlier?

"You know," Theo says, breaking me out of my gorgeousness induced stupor, "I never thought you'd be the kind of girl to use a spell to get out past curfew. I must be special if you're willing to risk the wrath of the headmaster."

I release the magic with my next breath and stand in front of him practically panting.

He notices my bag right away and his expression of casual indifference and easy play melts away into concern. "Yas? What's going on?"

I drop down in his desk chair and let the bag fall to the floor. "I have to go home tonight," I say. At his quick inhalation, I hurry on to say, "I want you to come with me. I know it's not smart and that we don't know each other well, but there's more going on in my life than I've let on. Things that I've been too scared to talk to you about but I'm ready to, now."

Concerned, Theo crosses the room and bends down

to take my hands in his. He's so strong. Much stronger than I gave him credit for, even when he'd been a stranger I admired across the cafeteria. "What is it? How can I help?"

I stare at him for a moment before huffing out a surprised laugh. "Just like that?"

He nods. "Just like that. Talk to me."

There is no hesitation. Hopefully he'll still be willing to hear me out once I get through the story. I draw in a breath so deep my chest aches.

And without waiting any longer, I tell him the truth about my family. About where I came from, my human sister and my mother who pushed me all my life to take my place in the caste of Clerics. "I'm sorry I haven't told you everything but according to Blaire, it's almost a crime to be a Cleric. I was scared." I bite down on my lower lip. "I'm coming clean, and it terrifies me."

Although Theo is still holding my hands, his face has gone blank. Not a carefully controlled mask this time, either, but genuine shock at the truth bomb.

"I didn't want you to shun me like everyone else did. I mean, hell, they don't even know me but they know enough to see I'm different. You and Blaire are the only ones who have looked at me like I'm a person, like I'm someone worth knowing." I tug my hands out of his grasp to wring them together, needing to crack my knuckles. Needing to hear something besides the harried sound of my own breathing and my voice, tension making me squeaky.

"I feel like me and my family are ruining things and this might bring you down with me but I had to share it.

With you." I hurry to get through everything and I know I'm rambling, trying to keep it together, but it's impossible to stop. "You mean a lot to me, Theo, and I understand if you don't want to be seen with me anymore, especially since I haven't helped you study one bit. You don't have to come with me tonight—"

I fall apart when he kisses me. His lips sear to mine, branding me, linking us together in this irrefutable way I feel throughout my body. The heat of his lips travels from my mouth all the way down my spine and thaws the ice in my stomach.

It's passionate. It's unforgettable. It's everything I've ever wanted and when he hauls me to my feet and plasters me against his chest, I forget. Only for a moment, I allow myself to disassociate from the pressing issues of my family and the big bad waiting for me.

Because Theo is here, and he's not running.

He's touching me and showing me, in this moment, that I really am worth it. His fingertips skim along my jawline, up to my hair, fisting it bring me closer yet. His opposite arm bands around my waist and wherever he touches me, I'm on fire.

I practically purr against his bare chest. Especially when I realize the hardness of him extends a lot lower than I thought.

"*Yas*," he says with a groan.

My name.

With a cry in the back of my throat, I link my arms around the back of his neck and tilt my head to deepen the angle of the kiss. Our tongues tangle together and there is nothing playful about this one. There is no hint of the explorative quality of our earlier kiss. There is only need, a sliding need, so bright it disguises everything else.

My body.

The things he does to me with just a kiss. I wonder what—

I lose the last strands of thought when Theo drops his hand from my hair to the side of my breast. He pauses there for half a heartbeat, waiting for my answer, and when I kiss him harder, he touches. He cups my breast in his palm, massaging it before tweaking my nipple between his thumb and forefinger. My grunt of approval spurs him on further and he delves his hand inside my shirt and beneath my bra, touching my skin.

Theo presses me against the desk and although I know there are important things beneath me, he doesn't seem to care. Not when he sweeps everything away and hoists me up onto the desktop, widening my legs and stepping between them.

His hand dips from my breast to southern territories and the heat between my legs is almost too much for me to bear. I break away to stare up at him.

It would be easy to go farther. To let his fingers explore my body the way I want him to. He pauses again overtop the fabric at my core with a question in his gaze. Whatever he sees on my face has him nodding once and shifting to place his hand on the top of my leg.

"We have time," he says, almost breathless. "Isn't that what I said before?"

"You did."

He pulls away to grab a shirt and drag it over his head. Without looking at me again, he tosses some things into a bag.

"I'm coming with you to help."

"I'm sorry," I start. "I don't want you to have to sacrifice your studies to help me. It was a mistake to drag you into this. Theo."

He's not paying any attention to me.

"If we hit the ground running tonight, then we can do something even more important than just theoretical bullshit." He glances over his shoulder at me. "Right, Yas? We can make an actual difference. We can save your family and your people."

I'm awestruck. "Yes," I say, swallowing hard. "Yes, we can."

CHAPTER
TWENTY

A lump forms in the back of my throat and I know that no matter how hard I try to clear it, it's stuck for good. *This man.* This man who knows everything about me now, who gave me a chance, is all in.

Tears prick the corners of my eyes and I know if I give myself even a second to think about how huge this moment really is, I'll break down.

He sees the tears and rather than telling me to buck up, or acting like they're an inconvenience, he kisses me again until I'm breathless for a completely different reason.

"We've got this," he assures me.

"I don't know how you're so calm. I'm freaking out. This is insane."

"It's pretty insane, yeah, but it's also a chance to actually do something. Stop." He barks out the words before I have a chance to say anything else. "Stop thinking you'll owe me for this."

"I never said that." I sound petulant.

"You don't have to. I see the guilt on your face. I'm going because I want to go. And because I want to protect you." He tosses me his cell. "Now call your sister and your roommate and tell them the deal. We're leaving in five."

Controlled Theo is even sexier than Poet Theo. I never would have guessed.

Rather than giving myself even the barest opportunity to overthink this, I use his cell to call the room. I'd told them to leave but knowing them, they're still there. Waiting to see what I've done and worrying.

Blaire answers on the second ring.

"We're all in," I tell her. "You guys head out. Theo and I are going to catch up to you on the road."

She blows out a breath. "I knew you were crazy, Yazzy, but this is beyond. Okay. So I'll ride with Remi and Atlas and we'll meet you and your boy-toy at the border. Is he—"

"Yes," I interrupt, sparing a look at Theo as he finishes with his sneakers and straightens. "We're fine. We're good."

Maybe my luck really has changed, I think as I hang up the phone. Being here with him, having Theo not only willing but able to help me in this moment, it's everything. It's a wish, it's a dream.

Let's hope it doesn't turn into a nightmare before we're done. The kind where he regrets helping and wants nothing to do with me.

"Let's go." Theo grabs my hand and we walk out of the room together, back toward his bike tucked in the spot in campus parking. The same spell I used to get here obscures us from view but there's nothing I can do, at least not at the moment with my brain turned to mush, to disguise the sound of the engine rattling.

Time to make a quick break for freedom.

We jump on the bike and dart off campus with the veil of night the only thing keeping us hidden.

I tell him where we need to go and hold on tight as he takes off. It's not going to be an easy trip. I remember the hours it took to get here the first time around and I'm not sure how far the border of the barrier extends outside of town. The odds are good it's going to take us hours to get home.

Luckily for us—again with the luck—the helmets are equipped with microphones to let us talk to each other during the drive. Theo asks me where we're going and I tell him, giving him more details.

Hoping we'll be able to make a difference.

My nerves keep me talking through most of the drive, filling in the missing pieces from my stories before.

Finally, after a couple of hours, we pull into the town adjacent to the border and stop at a gas station to fill up the tank. I rip my helmet off my head and drag in a deep pull of fresh air.

"Your face," Theo begins.

I offer him a grimace. "I'm scared shitless."

Even the air quality has changed this close to the border. It's thicker, heavier, and filled with the stench of things better left alone.

I've heard the stories of the Clerics and their demise.

Now, with my family potentially poised to pay the cost, what options do I have? I don't want to die. Not like this. Not without ever having experienced everything life can offer me. There are too many things in this life I've never had a chance to explore.

And Theo...

He says we have time, but he has no idea, not really, what I might have to do tonight to get the Horned God back where he belongs. We're running *out* of time, actually, and if I don't make it through tonight—

Am I okay letting things end between us on this note?

He smiles at me from the gas pump, a quick flash of a reassuring grin before it disappears in the navy and ebony evening.

If we had time, what would I give to him?

What would I ask from him in return? My thoughts flash once to the highlander romance novel and the great Seamus, the Scottish warrior. How he ravaged the love of his life.

I've never even thought about sex outside of a book before. Only in abstract terms, not about how I might be impacted because as a Cleric, it's not about intimacy. It's about power, and magic, and leading your coven with both of those things.

I've already been so selfish tonight.

I've already brought Theo into this. Still, I know absolutely nothing about how to make the first move. For *anything*. Only what I've picked up through Remi's romance novels.

What if I try to proposition him with my idea and he laughs in my face? There are a thousand reasons why this is a bad idea and I think about everything that can go wrong.

"You're right, we're close," he says once he's done filling up the bike. "We're almost to the border. I feel it. Where are we going?"

I place my hand on his arm before he has a chance to hop on the bike. "I want you to take us to the Yellow Ash Motel."

It's nearby and they rent by the hour. I know both of those things through my sister, who would have a conniption fit if she caught one whiff of what I planned to do. She told me about it in passing a few times when she and Atlas no longer felt comfortable sneaking around the library for the things they wanted to do to each other.

The things I want to do to Theo.

Decision made, once again.

Theo tilts his head to the side. "You want to go to a motel?" he asks.

I leave my hand on his arm, my helmet tucked under the opposite elbow, my needs plain to see even if I'm unable to voice them. Slowly, I nod. My mouth has gone dry again and a whole host of bees are swarming around inside of me. To combat them, I focus on the sensation of his hand on my breast, his tongue in my mouth. I focus on everything I know will come after those things.

And Theo sees what I'm trying to do.

"Are you sure?" he questions. "If that's what you really want, Yas, then you have to be sure because there is no going back." He steps closer, holding me when I start to shiver.

"Look..." I trail off. "I don't want to die without first living. Even if tomorrow comes and we both make it out and decide tonight is a mistake, it will be ours. Something I treasure." I admit. "If you're okay with it."

"I don't want you to feel like I'm taking advantage of you. These circumstances aren't—they're not—what I would have wanted for you. It's your first time?" He doesn't even need to ask the question, though.

My god, this is embarrassing.

"I want it to be with you," I reply. "I know this sounds crazy, but I've felt something for you since the first time I saw you." The embarrassment is real. I shrug, grabbing my opposite elbow to contain every large emotion inside. "I want *you*."

I'm barely able to look at Theo as he silently helps me onto the bike and guns the engine. "What's the address for the motel?" he asks through the helmet microphone.

I rattle off directions, my heart thudding a million miles an hour. The beat increases with each mile we take toward the hotel.

It's a small matter to slap some cash down on the front desk. To take the plastic key with the room number and make our way upstairs to the corner room, farthest away from the stairwell. It really is a rent by the hour kind of place.

Not what I might have wanted for us, if circumstances were different.

The door creaks open, the massive mattress of the king-sized bed taking up the majority of space. A tv sits propped against the opposite wall with thrift store paintings on the walls, hammered into the wood paneling. The comforter is done in shades of brown and orange to match the rest of the decor.

My blood is alive.

Theo gently closes the door behind me and flips the locks closed, the sounds ripping through my system like closely fired bullets. He steps close, his chest brushing against my back and his lips on my temple, my cheek. The side of my neck.

Goosebumps erupt.

"I've wanted you, too."

His whispered words are so low I barely catch them.

With a moan, I turn in his arms and loop my own around the back of his neck, dragging him down to press my lips to his. The kiss lasts for ten seconds before Theo bends, scooping me into his arms without breaking contact and carrying me over to the bed.

"I'll be gentle," he promises. "Since it's your first time."

"I have no idea what I'm doing." I'm not sure why I feel the need to offer the warning, either.

"We'll learn together."

I stare open mouthed at Theo as he positions himself over me, lowering himself between my legs. The contact is new, hot, and arousing as hell when I feel the hardness between his legs. Already he's ready and pushing against his jeans to get to me.

"It's your first time too?" I ask.

He chuckles lightly and nips at my chin. "No," he admits. "But it's my first time with you. That's what counts." Kissing me, he sweeps his tongue along the seam of my lips until I open for him. "It's the only thing that counts."

I lose myself in him and the kisses that taste like my dreams come true.

Theo is true to his word once again; gentle with me. Almost afraid to touch me as he peels off my shirt, then his. Skin to skin. Breath for breath, we're matched.

Until I don't want to go slow.

When his teeth are on my nipples and his hands gently probing the area between my legs, I don't want to go slow. I want to dive ahead and do everything I've ever read about. The nerves start to fade away underneath the warm, weighty haze of desire. His pants follow mine to the growing pile on the floor. It's natural. Nothing to be ashamed of and nothing to hide.

His fingers continue to probe my soft folds, paying close attention to one spot that feels absolutely fantastic. I'm almost too ashamed to reach for him. Until Theo drags my hand from his hip and places it at the base of his shaft.

"It's okay, Yas," he says. "It's okay."

I use my fingertips to tickle him, doing more, growing bolder when his breath hitches and a moan drags from the back of his throat. Until our kisses are filled with fire and lightning and he's breaking away to adjust himself better.

The first glimpse of him…

My eyes widen.

"Are you ready?" he asks.

Holding onto control by the smallest thread, keeping himself on a tight leash. For me. It's all for me.

I nod and slick my tongue along my lower lip, my mouth suddenly dry. "I'm ready."

I have to remind myself, *I'm ready*, even as I guide him to my entrance and he slowly sinks into me.

Tense seconds tick by while my body adjusts to his and the sensation of being filled. My fingers dig into his shoulders to stop him when he's halfway inside, my muscles gripping him. Inch by inch he pushes forward.

A gasp of pure anticipation escapes me once he's seated to the hilt.

Theo fills every inch. My knees grip both sides of his waist and his hands hold me in place as I take every inch of him. The pain lasts only moments before it shifts into discomfort. And finally after a few tense seconds where my body has to recalibrate, seconds where we stare at each other, drinking in the sensation of being together, I start to move my hips.

A slight demand to get him to move as well.

Theo draws himself out of me and I cry out when he jerks his hips forward and drives into me fully for a second time.

I grip his shoulders once he begins to take control. Trying to hold on for my life as we move together. It's more than I expected in every way, and the rest of the world melts away around us. There is only Theo, the odd sensation of being filled, and the energy crackling through my veins.

The most beautiful kind of tension. I wrap my legs around him to get into a more comfortable position and the movement drives him deeper yet. Arching my back brings my breasts up for him and he palms one, massaging it in time with his thrusts.

Before I know what's going on, he's pulled out of me with a cry of ecstasy. My head falls back to the mattress as Theo empties himself onto the shirt I hadn't realized he'd left on the other side of the mattress.

He works himself through his orgasm before turning back to me and kissing me, a searing kiss of possession this time.

"How do you feel?" he asks.

I shake my head. "My body isn't mine to control anymore. I can't move."

"Are you in any pain?"

"No." I reach for him and pull him back to me, trailing my fingers down the sweat slicked planes of his chest. "No, I'm not. Thank you."

Copper strands of hair stick to his forehead and I push them aside, tucking them behind his ears. "You don't have to thank me for something I wanted to do." This time his kiss is tender, sweet. "Yas…"

I snuggle next to his side and he wraps his arms around me, pulling me closer until my legs are sprawled over his. "Let's not talk about it now," I beg him. "I want to enjoy this. For a little while longer."

He tenses for a second before letting out a long

exhale, his muscles relaxing inch by inch. He marks little circles along my skin with his strong hands. "Anything you want."

"That was everything I wanted," I admit. Biting down on my lower lip.

The afterglow won't last long. When it fades, when I do what I have to do, who knows what else is going to change?

CHAPTER
TWENTY-ONE

It hurts to leave Theo alone in the room, sleeping with one arm flung casually above his head and his expression soft. Snoring slightly and to the point where the sound brings a smile to my face.

Gods, he's perfect.

Everything about him draws me still even as my body throbs from being imprinted with his. He'd done this for me. He'd come all this way, taken me for the first time, because I asked him.

Now, no matter how much it hurts, I have to do this for him.

I've endangered him enough.

It was a mistake to let him get this close, especially when I consider how much I don't know about the situation I'm walking into. There are a thousand variables and things that could go wrong and I'd been selfish to involve him. Too selfish.

Leaving him sucks and it's probably the best thing I've ever done for him.

I'm the worst.

I never should have gone to his room tonight.

No matter how great my body feels, no matter how my heart relaxes as I watch Theo sleep, I know I'm the worst because I put him in danger in the first place. Not only danger but then I took him back to this motel and I used him.

I shake my head to dislodge those thoughts.

No matter how guilty I feel for the first part, I refuse to let it impact the latter. What we'd done, how we'd made each other feel…

It is everything.

I'm not willing to risk him any more than I already have.

Quietly, I slip back into my pants and shirt, lacing my sneakers and grabbing my bag. Some of the bottles clink together and I tense, looking over my shoulder to see if the sound woke him.

Nope.

One final look over my shoulder when I get to the door assures me Theo is still asleep as I sneak out. Even the creaking of the hinges doesn't wake him. I say my silent goodbyes once I'm outside.

It's only going to be a few blocks of walking to get to the barrier.

It will be much faster on the bike but it's one step too far.

My chest tight, I breathe in the night air, heavy and cumbersome. Something is definitely wrong and it doesn't take a witch to understand that.

It's a sensation in the atmosphere, a tingle along the

skin warning of dark and unnatural things, as Remi said before. I grip the strap of my bag closer as though it will somehow protect me from the shadows stretching toward me. The Horned God is close.

Whatever spell he's used to leash the coven to his side ends tonight. My footsteps echo eerily, the sound trailing me down the sidewalk. Even the night creatures have quieted this close to the border.

At least now I have a name to put to the shadows I'd seen from the corner of my eyes ever since I got to Andora. The niggling sensation of eyes on the back of my neck is real and now I'm going to face them head on.

Jaw clenching, muscles tense, my teeth rattle together and a chill takes up residence in my blood.

The determination does nothing against the ruthless swell of nerves eating at my insides. Rather than give into them, I keep my gaze ahead, each step wooden down the sidewalk until I reach the edge of the barrier.

It's nothing you can see with the naked eye. More a feeling, a sensation warning anyone to stay the hell away from whatever this is. I close my eyes and tune into the world around me, seeing the barrier as a night-black and star-studded thickening of the air. A ripple in time and space. My mother's signature, I realize with a start.

Whatever else might have happened to her, she had enough time to throw up this protection around the town center, to keep the coven contained. To keep the humans out.

Well, however many of them were lucky enough to

get out before the spell took hold.

Tears burn the backs and corners of my eyes.

It's time.

Glancing around, there's no hint of the others. They should have been here by now, especially with the stop I made. It's better, though. I'm all the more grateful for it because I don't want Blaire involved.

I definitely don't want Remi and Atlas to come with me for this because they're human.

Human and breakable.

My fight, my terms. My town.

"Time to face me head on, you bastard," I mutter out loud.

I square my shoulders and take one step through the barrier despite every sense screaming at me to turn tail and run. *Run.* There's a lot of pushback those first few paces through the barrier, the magic fighting against me to keep me out. Hands in front of me, I keep going, pushing the magic out of the way to make room for me, until I'm through to the other side.

The town center is completely dark and silent.

"Hello? Is anyone here?"

Much to my surprise, vines in various shades of ebony and midnight have risen to cover most of the buildings. There are no birds or bats calling out to each other here. No animal noises or even the usual rustling of the wind.

Dead silence.

If anyone had gotten trapped inside the barrier who didn't belong, they had to be smart enough to hide. To lock themselves in their houses and board the windows.

My footsteps echo eerily as I make my way toward the ruins of the library where, I figure, I'm more likely to run into the possessed coven members.

Focus.

There's no sense in worrying about what might go wrong. Or, more precisely, what will likely go wrong, because I might be book smart but that's a whole lot different from using my powers for combat.

Rounding the last corner, my focus isn't on the shell of the library or the crumbling brick walls. It's completely focused on the members of the coven standing stock still in a circle on the outskirts of the forest. They've congregated on the small square of grass with the dark press of trees an ominous backdrop to this whole thing.

I barely hear a breath.

They stand as still as statues, with even the light of the moon and stars overhead blotted out. Each of them faces the center of the circle, arms outstretched.

There is no movement and no light. No candles or sacred flame to guard against the darkness. The members of the coven have their faces tilted up to the sky and their arms tense in front of them, waiting.

Waiting for what?

Hardly daring to think, I take a step closer, glancing around the area. The Horned God isn't anywhere nearby but I sense him, at the edges of my awareness while he waits to strike. A collective inhalation sounds louder than an explosion and I jerk my attention back to the coven circle.

As one, they step to the side to reveal the hidden

space at the center of their circle. And there, seated by a hollowed-out tree trunk in the space between bodies, is my mother.

"Mom."

She's okay. She's alive—no one has absorbed her power yet. I hurry forward, stopping when I'm close enough to see the truth.

She's been affected the same way as the others.

Her attention falls on me, her eyes glowing green. She swings her arm right and the other coven members follow her lead until they are all pointing at me.

Oh no. This isn't good.

My feet freeze to the ground, more out of fear than any kind of spell work and the rest of me freezes like ice. Frost has my bones threatening to crack and the panic inside of me turns to outright terror.

What do I have with me that can break a spell of this magnitude? Mentally I try to think about everything I've got, nothing sticking. Nothing that will make a difference.

That's when Mom starts to chant.

I hear the crinkle of growing things in fast-forward before I see any actual plant growth, and seconds later vines sprout from my mother's feet. They shift, rolling over each other like a pit of snakes, and cover the ground around the witches in a circle. The vines circle their ankles, climbing up pant legs.

Her chanting is summoning the Horned God.

And when he appears, we're all done for.

"No!" The word erupts from my mouth right as I lurch forward. "Mom, don't do it! Stop chanting."

I sprint to the circle, tugging at the vines to break their hold on the coven members. They're iron and unbreakable, growing thicker even as I watch.

I've got to get to my mom.

"Mom, stop," I yell. "You have to stop! Don't call him here. He can't appear!" My shouting bounces right off her. I grab those vines, using every ounce of strength to break them and do the impossible. They're too strong.

They seem to get thicker the longer she chants and I have to step back before they wrap around *my* ankles and legs.

"Mom, don't do it!" I lose my voice, power making it hard to draw in a breath. My throat constricts and I collapse to the ground. Magic pulsates up and around me, leaving me unable to do anything except gawk in horror as the Horned God steps out of the hollow tree trunk with a loud shriek designed to rattle the earth. Dirt erupts from between his legs, each of them covered in fur and ending in cloven hooves.

His body unfolds, muscles unnaturally swollen and his mask no longer that. The creepy animalistic features of the mask are now his face, the man beneath it lost to the swirling power he'd stolen.

Distorted cheekbones jut out from his face, gleaming canines lengthening into fangs as his lips peel back from his mouth. Horns curl out of the back of his head and grow, shifting into points that drip moss. His eyes are black, wicked, and somehow glowing in the lack of light.

No longer a man but a demon carved from his own selfishness.

The scent of smoke fills my nostrils and once again I'm back at the bonfire, the people no longer dancing around the flames but forced to move. Forced to keep moving in supplication to him as he drains them of everything they have to give.

They won't stop until they're dead.

They were too late to stop the rogue Cleric before he decided to step out of his lane. Too late to do anything except bow to his wishes. Just like I'm too late to stop him now.

In a single sudden shifting movement, somehow terrifyingly loud, the coven, every single member, turns to me at the same time and stares. Their eyes are glazed over, as eerie a sight as the monstrous god rising out of nothingness, out of nature, and towering over the crouched figure of Mom.

Through it all she's still chanting. Still laying the foundation for this *thing's* reign in this world after being banished for so long. Except she's not the Cleric he wants. Not by a long shot. Her time has ended and mine is just beginning. Or about to.

Wouldn't have been if I hadn't interrupted the ascension ceremony and interrupted his plans for me.

A bright red tongue slips out to slick over those canines.

I hear his voice inside my head, not even remotely human anymore.

Bring her to me.

CHAPTER
TWENTY-TWO

I hear his voice in my head in a bastardized version of the connection I share with Gus. I grind my teeth to force out the Horned God, bending over at the waist with my hands over my ears like it will somehow keep him out.

It does not.

The tone is so powerful, so ancient, I drop to my knees Even when I know the creature in front of me used to be a man I can't stop the fear, the realization that this is a beast so much greater than anything else in this world. Once, he was a flesh-and-blood witch with power of his own, before he stole from others and it twisted him.

Now he is the embodiment of our downfall, and I'm the one who brought him here.

Those bodies making up the outer ring of the coven all take a step as one toward me, the sound of their feet against the ground a low drumbeat. One right after the other.

It shoots straight through me and spurs me into action like nothing else can. I lose sight of Mom, vowing to come back to her later, to help if I can.

If.

With a yelp I stand, sprinting in the opposite direction with the weight of too many eyes on my back.

No way in hell I'm letting them catch me!

I don't need to look over my shoulder to know they're giving chase. Under his spell, they have no choice but to obey his command to retrieve me. And if the Horned God wants me then they'll do whatever it takes to deliver his prize.

My feet pound the pavement. Where's the best place for me to run? To hide? What do I have with me that I can use to buy time?

There has to be something in my pack to put an end to this.

I have crystals and my magic talismans, including an Evil Eye to absorb negativity, but those aren't going to be enough to act as a defense and slow the coven members down. Anything stronger runs the risk of killing them, though.

It's a hard line to toe.

"Yasmine."

The voice is a whisper in the wind.

"We're coming for you."

They speak with one voice and my stomach drops.

My numb fingers fumble on the zipper to the bag, dragging it down far enough to get my hand inside. I grab a bag of herbs and crystals I've charmed to start a small burning fire wherever it lands.

"Stay back!" I warn.

I toss it over my shoulder and the heat of the fire burns my back for a second before I dart forward and leave my pursuers in the dust.

The footsteps keep coming. The small fire does nothing to slow down the possessed coven members. The bottles in my bag clink together while I grab for something else to distract them. A spell and careful aim send tree limbs from the giant oak on my right crashing down to the ground.

They're fast, ruthless.

"Leave me alone!"

I mutter the words for the invisibility spell, turning a corner around the courthouse and stopping to see if they'll continue. The footsteps slow but they don't stop.

I'm trying my best and making no headway.

I glance down at my arm. There isn't enough light to reflect off me, so even though the spell has worked, I'm still here. Still visible. Blowing out a breath, I keep walking, purposely slowing my steps to make less noise. It's a risk, a pointed and calculated one. And I'm not sure how it will pay off given the Horned God's powers. His worshippers might be able to see past elementary cloaking magic.

What else do I have?

Crouching over my bag, I dig into the depths, rooting around for a crystal to absorb negativity. I grab the Evil Eye, looping the rope around my wrist to keep it in place.

"Come out, little witch, come out!" one of the coven members calls.

"We're not going to hurt you," adds another.

They have the same cloyingly sweet tone I don't trust for a single second. The footsteps grow closer until they stop. Directly in front of me.

The cloaking spell fails, guttering out, and I feel it disintegrating before I stand, pointing out with the amethyst crystal wand in my hand.

Magic words.

Good intent.

I know my Latin and I know the spells. I'm ahead in my class even though I came in late. I'm not going to let this fear stand in the way of my survival.

A blank gaze lands on me as I finish the spell and the magic ripples out toward them, a dark tendril of fog lifting from the woman's chest.

And the magic keeping the coven member trapped under the Horned God's spell disappears for a moment. Blankness shifts away into sheer terror and we lock eyes, right before my power flickers away and *his* spell snaps back into place.

"Oh, shit."

Wand still in hand, I bolt again. I've got a potion in the bag that is supposed to clear the mind. Don't I? I made it up on a whim right after Theo and I met at the statue, thinking it might help him even if I didn't agree to help him.

If I managed to get through to the witch for one second with the wand absorbing the negativity, then maybe the potion will go the extra mile. Okay, the amethyst and my intention. I want them to be free.

I want my mom back. I want my coven back.

SPELLING DISASTER

The potion is in my bag somewhere but stopping again is stupid. I shuffle through the depths as I jog, looking for the slender blue glass bottle with the cork top. And when I turn around a second time, it's not just any coven member behind me, it's Lark.

Her eyes are glazed but her lips lift in a feral grin.

"Found you," she murmurs.

I throw the potion directly at the center of her chest. The cork pops out of the top and the liquid inside splashes onto her skin and clothing. Just a minute, that's all I need to get her to call off this chase.

"Listen to me, Lark, you've got to stop," I say as she shakes the liquid off like a dog. She twists her head, pain flashing across her face. "Whatever he's doing to you, you have to fight it. You're stronger than he is! We can't let him get away with this."

I shuffle backward as I speak.

Grunting, the high priestess turns to me. "Find the book," she manages to get out. "Return him to it by sacrificing that which you love most. Only then can we all be free."

She doubles over, grunting in pain, fighting. She's fighting against the thrall but the more seconds tick by, the harder it is for the high priestess to continue against the press of power. It's growing stronger and those vines slither along the sidewalk reaching out for me.

Sacrifice what I love the most?

What the hell does it mean?

An image of Theo instantly flashes through my mind and I balk. I can't hurt him. I won't. I refuse to do it because there has to be another way. Any other way.

"How do I get the Horned God back in the book?" I ask the priestess. "Please, tell me. You have to know. You have to have some kind of spell that will trap him. Help me find a way to free us all."

Yasmine, listen to me.

I hazard a step closer before a voice sounds through my head. Not my own, though.

Gus appears at my feet with his whiskers twitching. He works his little white front feet together in a prayer.

You've got to follow me. I know where we can find the book.

"You were supposed to stay with Remi."

When I bend to scoop Gus up, he darts away down the sidewalk in the opposite direction.

Lark stays rooted to the spot with sweat glistening along her forehead.

You're wasting time! Come on.

If Gus is here without Remi, then it's for a reason.

I take off after him, not surprised when he leads me to the remains of the charred library. Sadness flickers inside me for only a moment before I push it aside and follow him through the stacks.

Soon the unbearable weight of everything I've lost threatens to push me into a pile of ash. These are the ruined stacks I'd once called home. All the books my coven had treasured. I memorized the number of steps it took to get to any section, to go anywhere.

The library is mine, and this is what it's come to.

"How do you know the book hasn't been destroyed? It's got to be a pile of dust at this point." I stop dead in my tracks and Gus flicks a look over his shoulder at me, his whiskers twitching.

It's magic. It's here somewhere. Do you remember where you dropped it?

Not particularly, but it's worth a shot to walk the paths where I'd last shoved the book. The coven will be here shortly. I'm surprised they aren't already. And the likelihood of finding the book is slim. If that's the only place to imprison the Horned God then he more than likely already has it in his possession. To keep it from me.

If I listen carefully, I hear the coven members growing closer. Beneath the odd silence of the town inside the barrier, it's almost like I hear them screaming. Screaming beneath the weight of whatever thrall they're under and begging me to free them.

Great.

The pressure is enough to give me a heart attack as I pick my way along the destroyed valleys between the shelves.

They've got me surrounded and there's no way out. Claustrophobia sets in and makes breathing difficult. A few more paces and I should be there. The shelves are mangled, books everywhere and ash filling the air with each step. I choke, swallowing down on the sound unless I want to give away my position. And just as I've been found out, ducking behind a blackened shelf, the footsteps pass me by.

Gus climbs my pant leg and nestles on the strap of the bag next to my face.

We've got to hurry.

"I'm glad you found me," I tell him. "Where do we go from here?"

You're doing it. You're retracing your steps. Stop giving into the fear and listen for it. He makes a good point. *You found it once before. What does the book feel like? It draws you.*

He's right again, and once I'm sure I no longer hear the screaming of the coven members, I crouch low and jog away.

Feel the book…

It found me the first time. It lured me over to the shelves where it had been hidden and called to me with such clarity it might as well have said my name. It's here somewhere. Underneath the footsteps and the silent screams, energy pulses.

Finally, I move closer to where the book should have been on the shelf, in the back, where I'd placed it the first time. It's there in perfect condition. Right where I'd left it, without so much as a char or a bit of ash on the cover. The letters gleam in the dullness and the writing on the cover is finally clear despite the strange cursive lettering.

Of The Merlin Order.

Gus reads it at the same time I do.

Whatever it means, this is the only way to trap the Horned God. I've got the book in hand and ignore the zap of electricity shooting through my fingertips when I touch the cover.

This is it. This is what started all this trouble and although I'd never had a problem opening a book before, there's a first time for everything. Along with the electricity, a strange sense of calm pervades my system. If I have the book then it's only a matter of time before I can put the Horned God back. I have to believe it. I have to feel inside of myself that I'm able and worthy of this. Otherwise, what's the point?

Gus and I make our way out of the ruined maze of the library and back toward the center of town.

The path is open and clear for us.

This meeting is overdue but at least now I'm done running.

"Come on out! Don't send your lackeys to find me this time," I yell, knowing he'll hear me.

"Come and face me instead of hiding behind the coven like the coward you are, you little chicken shit!"

There's a supernatural sense of the surreal to the moment and to the belief I can overcome all of this and leave unscathed. A small part of me wonders if I actually feel that way or if it's the way *he* wants me to feel.

Especially when the Horned God reveals himself, stepping into my path, his eyes lit with an internal fire.

"And right into my trap you've fallen, little one," he says out loud. "You're made this too easy for me."

CHAPTER
TWENTY-THREE

The whole *feeling myself* thing? An illusion. I realize now he used me to grab the book. Not without someone actually handing it to him and I'm the only witch who can, considering I'd been about to ascend to Cleric. Shit.

"Get back in the book," I tell the Horned God with false bravado.

Gus squeaks and retreats into my bag to hide.

"I'm not going anywhere, Yasmine."

His voice is the elemental power of thunder, the crashing tides. It's unearthly and powerful at the same time and listening to him it's hard to remember he'd been human once. A person just like me.

I keep my attention on him even as the rest of the coven separates themselves from the vines and the shadows. They surround us as the Horned God cackles.

"You summoned me here, remember? This is all from your magic. But you know that," he finishes.

My magic? No. I'd been about to set my magic aside to join the caste of Clerics.

That's where he began too.

Like me.

The Horned God snaps his fingers and the vines grow around us until they form a canopy overhead, a dome to keep us contained within the barrier.

"Maybe your friends and family need to know your little secret," he continues. "Don't you think?"

All eyes fall to me again in a sort of military movement. And for a moment, just a tiny moment, their eyes clear and they focus on me with a clarity that I know is his doing as well.

"Tell them, Yasmine, how *you* are responsible for this torture, for the destruction of everything they have held sacred." His voice drops to an all too human purr.

I bite down on my lip and refuse to answer.

It's not me. I'm not the one. I'm nobody.

"Perhaps you need a bit more to push you to answer, then. To act."

The Horned God steps back with his arm raised and the vines part, dragging three new bodies into the circle around us. No, I correct with horror dawning, four.

He has Blaire. Remi, Atlas, and…Theo.

No. No, no.

I'm too scared to move, and standing in place is nearly impossible with the way my blood thickens and shifts inside me like insects.

"The destitution has to count for something," the Horned God says. "The reason you were confined to this library, this place, is because they *all* knew you were too powerful. The one destined to ascend to the highest position of Clerics known. To sit at my side."

I can't tear my eyes away from Theo, but staring at him for too long will only show how important he is to me. Although I suppose the Horned God has already figured it out.

"I will never sit at your side. I refuse to ally myself with a man like you. That's right, a man. You only got to this position by stealing power from others, not out of your own merit."

There is nothing human about him anymore, not even the small shred of humanity I thought I'd heard in his voice.

"That's fine. Your agreement is not necessary. I only want your magic."

There's no warning of his impending attack until he sends a ball of fire flinging straight at me. Screaming, I duck, hands going overhead with the book a terrible shield. His attack lands true and the fire sets the book alight until I'm left holding a handful of ashes.

"No." The word explodes out of me in a harsh and burning whisper.

The ashes from the book, his prison, slowly sift through my fingers.

That's it, we're done. There's no chance of getting him back in now. He's destroyed his own prison and I let him. So easily. So fast.

If I'm really as powerful as he thinks I am then I wouldn't have allowed him to do such a thing. What can

I do now that the only thing that can contain him is destroyed?

I'm helpless. Whatever magic I'm supposed to have has failed me now.

"Yasmine!"

I shake my head, the wind picking up around us, blowing the leaves of the vines but not dislodging them.

"Yas, remember your training!" It's Mom's voice, but that's impossible. She's still under his spell.

The Horned God controls everyone just like he controlled me and got me to bring the book right to him.

"Your training, the books, the portals. The book destroyed was once created by a witch like you. You have to—"

She cuts off on a gargle as the spell is reactivated and clicked into place, keeping her silent again.

"What are you going to do, little witch?" The Horned God squares off against me and the pavement beneath his feet shakes with each step he takes.

"Do you really believe you're capable of facing me and winning? Or is it just the delusional mind of yours? The one who prefers to live in fantasies rather than reality? All your power, wasted," he continues.

I cast a hand out in front of me, a spell for protection rippling out from my outstretched palm and lashing against the Horned God. He glances down at the spot where the spell hit and bounced off of him. His eyes are indulgent when he looks back at me.

"Is that all you've got?"

I follow up with the amethyst wand, tucked and

hidden in my back pocket. Dark violet light shoots out at him and wraps around one of his wrists. The force sends him back a single step before he manages to find his balance again.

His hit slams into the side of my head hard enough to have stars dancing in front of my vision.

I lift the wand just in time to ward off his next hit heading for my other temple. The ringing in my ears has me unbalanced.

I might be able to turn metal into gold, but can I turn a man into stone?

The pieces of various spells jumble together in my head until they finally form a cohesive picture. I'd accidentally turned Gus into something else. Transformation. Transfiguration.

Latin syllables flow out of me as I work the spells together into something new, twisting the wand through the air, forming sigils between our bodies.

"Cute trick," the Horned God replies.

He's confident until he tries to take a step and his hoof does not rise from the ground. The vines might be his trick, but this is mine. The ground rises to engulf him, his muscles hardening and turning to stone.

His smile is gone, features shifting into a terrifying frown. I keep the pressure on him, sending the magic up to his knees and the loincloth.

"It's a trick that's going to land you on your ass," I whisper.

Unfortunately for me, getting cocky is not the solution.

Summoning his strength, the Horned God lifts his leg at last and cracks the spell holding him.

His answering hit sends me on my backside and pain shoots from my tailbone up my spine. For every bit of ground I gain, he knocks me back. Again, and again.

"Enough of this," he snaps.

I've got the spell to turn him to stone ready to go again, if only I can get access to the deepest parts of the well of my power. No time. Not enough time, I think in a flash, the seconds disappearing as the Horned God swivels and reaches out for a body behind him.

He's going for Theo.

Adrenaline courses through me and without thought, without a plan, I grab my book from the bag at my feet.

"You can't have him!" I scream.

The spell is one I've utilized a thousand times to send me into the story and as I toss out my favorite highlander romance novel, it sucks Theo into it through a bright portal of light. His mouth rounds in a plea before he disappears.

At least in there he'll be safe.

"If I can't have your boyfriend then I'll take the others."

The Horned God goes after Blaire, and Atlas, his fist raised to smash them with the long branch materializing in his hand.

"You're not going to touch any of them." I repeat the spell and suck each one of them into the novel with Theo.

Until the Horned God takes Remi by the throat.

"Poor girl. Always a step behind and not realizing when she's been beat," he says.

Choking, Remi reaches up to grip his wrist, to get him to let her go. Her feet kick against the open air.

He snaps the fingers of his opposite hand and releases the rest of the coven from their positions.

"Attack her." It's a simple command.

They launch into an attack, fueled by his magic, and I have no more time to pull tricks out of a hat. Summoning every bit of power at my disposal, I grow my own barrier around us, me and the Horned God and Remi to keep the coven out. The shield shimmers into place with the glow of a setting sun and, even more surprisingly, holds.

The coven beats against the barrier and casts spells of their own, to blast through, to find chinks in my defense. I grit my teeth against the exhaustion and the effort needed to maintain the protective circle.

"Yes, strong," the Horned God murmurs behind me. "As I knew you would be."

"My mother made sure I was more than prepared for my ascension," I tell him. A muscle ticks in my jaw.

"Please, do show me more of what you can do," he pushes. "I'd love to see more of your action in motion, to get a better feel for what I'll soon have for my own."

I ignore him, focusing on my sister. "Remi! Now!"

She nods through her panic and a slight glimmer of sweat has her face shining and pale.

She knows what I'm talking about. She always does. She can read my mind better than anyone else I know.

"Do it now!"

She doesn't waste another moment. Her one hand is free, thanks to the Horned God's posturing, and she reaches into the pocket of her button up shirt and drags out her favorite lighter. The one she always keeps hidden on her to keep Mom from knowing Remi smokes on occasion.

She lights the Horned God on fire.

Part of him, at least, the lichen hanging from his horns that are closest to her. As the lichen go up in flames, he releases her, dropping her to the ground.

With Remi free, I toss her out of the circle with a thought. Magic sends her careening past the golden and glowing protective wall toward the open romance novel where she's sucked inside.

She's safe. Finally, she's safe. And with her gone—

"You focus on me," I tell the Horned God. "This is between us."

His eyes narrow as he stares at me, their depths bottomless and expansive, so dark they threaten to pull me into them, where I'd never escape again.

"What do you think you're going to do? Just because you've thrown your toys away doesn't mean this ends well for you, Yasmine. Your magic will be mine."

My magic. The part of me I've always loved the most.

"I'm told that in order to contain you, I'll have to sacrifice that which I love the most," I tell him. "It's not even a question."

With everyone else safe, that only leaves one more thing...

I toss back my head and the scream that rips from

inside of me is tortured. Because to save the people I love permanently, I have to sacrifice my magic. The pool of it inside of me, the always bubbling cauldron of power simmering at any given time, for me to use, is there when I reach for it.

Focusing on it now, I push everything I have toward the Horned God to create a barrier around him. Tick, tock. The protective circle keeping the coven at bay starts to fall, diminishing as the full brunt of my magic slams into the Horned God.

He's yelling, but I barely hear him above the roar in my ears. The draining sensation coming from inside of me and the voice in my head begging me to stop. It's not as loud as the voice telling me to push for more. To give him everything I've got.

A sacrifice.

It was never a choice.

Never something I had to think about.

The barrier around the Horned God holds even as he lifts claw-tipped hands to pound against it. Not for a second do I consider failure. With the barrier growing, the coven pushing toward me, the Horned God grows smaller and smaller. The power of the circle radiates outward and the smaller he becomes, the less his spell over the others holds.

It breaks, shatters, and they slow with their fingertips only inches away from grabbing me.

Sweat breaks out along my forehead, down my back, on my stomach and under my arms. The effort of taking every bit of fantastical power inside of me and forcing it to become energy in 3D takes its toll.

"You want it?" I manage. "Here it is."

All of it.

And it's too much for him.

The ground beneath our feet rumbles and trees topple, careening toward us and missing by *that much*. The library ruins behind me combust again as flames roar up toward the sky and the dome of the barrier above our heads. Still, I focus on him, containing him and all of his ill intent.

I grit my teeth and push more. Every last drop of what I have. It has to be enough.

A body presses against my back as a familiar scent pervades my awareness. Mom. With her free, she's protecting my back, keeping me safe while I do this.

It's hard, physically and mentally. I feel the sensation of my power slipping away like I've lost control of millions of threads that all fit together. I have to let them go even knowing they'll never be in my hands again and the loss it entails.

When I have him down to the size of a dime and my power is down to the bare dregs, I collapse.

Mom places her hand on my shoulder. A comforting presence and a plea for me to not stop. To keep going. Much to my surprise, the other coven members do the same. One by one they lend me their magic to help defeat the Horned God.

Magic rushes into me and takes up the space where mine used to be in a wave of warmth. It's temporary, which makes this all the more bittersweet. Soon even the dregs of my magic are gone and the Horned God is nothing but a wisp of smoke trailing an inch above the ground.

"Mom…"

I trail off and with the smoke contained in a circle of glowing light, courtesy of the coven, she captures the Horned God in a blessed mason jar and seals him inside.

CHAPTER
TWENTY-FOUR

For a few beats, I barely breathe.

The vines sink back into the ground before disappearing entirely, gone as though they'd never been, the spell broken.

"Mom?" Trembling, I reach for her, tears finally breaking free when she grabs me in a tight hug.

"You did it," she murmurs into my hair. "Oh, Yasmine, you did it."

"Is it really you?" I lean back to inspect her. Her eyes aren't glowing green but how the hell do I know if she's still under his spell? "Talk to me."

Her lips thin. "You seriously want me to prove myself to you right now?" she asks.

There's enough venom in her voice to convince me and I hug her back, hard enough to wrench the air from her lungs. "I missed you."

The coolness of the jar presses to my back. "I missed you, too, my girl."

"Yasmine! Oh my goodness." I break away from

Mom only to have Lark grab me in another hug, her heartbeat more than evident through the thin material of her ceremonial cloak.

The spell really is broken.

Everyone is back to their normal selves.

Having the coven thank me, profusely and relentlessly, sits wrong. I'm not used to the praise and not altogether sure it's deserved, considering the massive amount of help I had. Not to mention the near failure where we barely escaped from the Horned God.

"We never should have treated you the way we did," Lark admits. She casts sad blue eyes on me, her pale hands reaching out as though to push the hair from my eyes and falling back to her side a moment later. "We were wrong."

Now that one, I'll take.

Rather than automatically blowing her off, or telling her not to worry about it, I frown. "You treated me terribly," I reply. "You kept me on the outskirts of the coven my entire life, and when it counted, no one bothered to listen to me."

"You're right. We've always treated you as something to fear rather than embracing you the way we should have. Nothing we do now will be able to erase the past," she continues. "Just know we're grateful. So grateful for what you've done for us. And I speak for everyone when I say we are sorry. We owe you."

Mom rubs my shoulder with her hand and Gus climbs my pant leg to squat on my other side, a mouse barrier in case the rest of the coven decides to be too affectionate again. To be too apologetic. He senses my emotional overwhelm better than any other supportive presence.

"We'll try to do better," the high priestess insists. "From here on out, we'll be better."

Eli steps up and the tightening crowd of bodies around me shifts back a little at his presence. "Our deep-rooted suspicion of the Clerics is to blame. Not an excuse, but the truth. We ostracized you and your family, Yasmine," he explains. "We should have told you the truth from the start."

"I don't want to hear any more of your apologies. It's a little too late for it," I try to say, to stop him before he goes any further.

"Know we have a long way to go to make amends for all that has happened. I hope you'll return to us and give us a chance to make this right." He offers a smile instead.

I step closer to Mom. "I don't want your apologies, and I don't want your amends. I just want to get back to Andora and my life, with this behind me," I admit. Mom stiffens and I turn to her, speak to her rather than the rest of them. "I want to start figuring out who I am without a shadow overhead, or anyone else's expectations. For me." I'm so damn tired. And it's past time for her to hear me.

What I want.

Who I want.

Oh, shit. "Theo!" I call out his name. "I need to talk to Theo." The energy causes the romance novel pages to shiver.

In the next breath, the book opens and out jumps

the man in question. Except he's not the way I left him. He's wielding a sword, hefting it high overhead, and is fully dressed as a highlander. His sneaker and jeans ensemble has been replaced with a red and green tartan kilt and his hair is long and flowing, giving me serious old-school Fabio vibes. My mouth goes dry before instantly watering so much that I'm worried I might drool. In fact, Theo would give the infamous romance model a run for his money.

His wild eyes fall on me and he swings the sword in a wide arc. "Everyone get back! Back! Yasmine." Two steps and suddenly I'm in his arms with his sword way too close for comfort. Well, one of his swords, the one made of steel. "Are you okay?"

He checks me everywhere, and I have to catch my breath, grabbing him to keep myself grounded.

"I'm fine," I tell him, rising on my toes to kiss him. "We did it, Theo. We defeated the Horned God. Now we need to find some place to put him." I would rather not look at the jar Mom holds in both hands.

Theo slowly comes back to himself, shaking off the thralls of his highland experience. His posture relaxes and his tautness melts away with each touch of his fingers along my cheek, neck, shoulder. Each kiss.

"You know, I might actually have an idea. For a good place to hide him. The best place because he will be hidden in plain sight. You remember the Merlin statue on campus?" Theo proposes.

Oh my god, he's right. The original book had "The Merlin Order" written on the cover. It's poetic irony at its finest.

The statue had been someone forgotten by time, forgotten by everyone. Called Merlin because his name had been lost to history. Suddenly I realize the humble looking Cleric founder whose likeness is forever memorialized in the statue was actually the Horned God.

"Yas?" Theo drags me under the shelter of his arm when I start to shake.

"I'm fine," I manage to get out.

He'd fallen by trying to rise. Above his station. Above everyone. He'd paid the price. If there's even a sliver of awareness left, being trapped in the jar will be his punishment until the end of time.

Saying none of this out loud because I have a gut feeling no one will understand how sad it makes me, I smile up at Theo. "That's the perfect place to put him, you're right. Damn good idea."

He stares at me for a minute longer, blinking, before his usual mischievous smile is back in place. "Are you ready to go home?" he asks. "I want to sleep for a million years in my own bed, and wake up to have breakfast with my girlfriend."

Home. I'm not sure how or when, but somewhere along the line, the academy campus came to mean much more to me than I ever realized.

I nod, linking my hand through Theo's and shaking him slightly until he drops the sword. "Sounds like an amazing idea. I'm ready."

"You're going to leave so soon?" Mom asks, with only a hint of ire.

"Mom, I'm happy to be back. And I'm happy

everything is normal again. But there's so much to learn at the academy. I want to stay there," I tell her.

"But your magic… You've used it to trap the Horned God."

"Not all of it," Eli says, stepping closer to Mom's side. "Her magic may be depleted right now, dimmed, but it can never truly be erased. It may take some time, but as long as magic dwells inside her, she'll always be welcomed at the academy."

I don't need him to agree with me. Still, it helps, having him as backup.

"And I want to stay with Theo." Then brace for impact.

Mom pinches the bridge of her nose. "You're telling me you want to go back to school because of a guy you just met?"

Gus presses close to my cheek and I press close to Theo. "Not just for him, although he's a definite perk."

"Jaime, with Yasmine at the academy, she can ensure the Horned God will never return to wreak havoc again," Eli continues.

Her mouth opens and closes while she gets herself under control. There's no way Mom is going to fight with me with the High Priest and Priestess watching her.

Finally, she thrusts her arms into the air. "Fine! Leave me." But the thin line of her lips twitches and I know she's hiding her grin.

I'd go back to the academy whether Eli wanted me to or not. It's not the right time to kick up a fuss, though. So I shoot him a grateful smile, a little tighter around the edges than the one I give Theo, and stuff my exhaustion aside.

The pages of the romance novel ripple again in an invisible breeze and Blaire, Remi, and Atlas all spring out of the book dressed as characters from the story. My roommates' hair is in knots around her face and she has bags under her eyes.

Glancing around, she pulls it together first.

"Girl, *never* send me into a book again. How long were we in there?" she asks.

"Only for a few minutes. Twenty at most," I tell her.

"Well, for us, it was a whole ass week and I am happy it's over." She sags. "I'm over this whole thing without modern conveniences and bathing in lakes."

She might look like she's been put through the ringer but Remi and Atlas appear almost regal. From their bearing to their clothes, I can see how the balance of power was shifted during their trip inside the story.

The magic can be fickle. It's hard to say who you'll end up being.

"What's this, now?" Mom gestures toward Atlas with her nose, seeing how close the two of them stand. "Both my daughters have been involved with boys and no one wanted to tell me?"

"This is my boyfriend." Remi sounds strong, and only a little Scottish. "Atlas, this is my mother, Jaime. Mom...it doesn't matter what you say. We're together and we're not going to break up just because you don't approve." She loops her arm through his. "He's mine."

The look on her face dares Mom to argue.

I give Mom credit. She shows no sign of her usual

reaction as she walks up to the two of them and draws them into a hug. "Remi, you have my blessing," she says. "I'm going to stay out of your life. Both of your lives. Okay?"

My sister blinks, confused, before returning the hug. "It's okay, Mom, it's fine. We're safe. You can stop with the panic now."

I shake my head and Theo tugs at me. "The bike is parked at the edge of the barrier," he tells me softly. "Are you ready to go?"

If he's surprised by me having a familiar, he doesn't show it. Not when Gus gives him the appraising eye and ducks into my bag for the ride.

"Yes," I agree. "I'm more than ready to go."

I want to sleep for days. Weeks. I want to sleep with Theo and wake up in his arms where I know for sure I'll be safe.

Mom shifts her attention to the barrier around the town and closes her eyes. She breathes out slowly once, twice. Eventually the barrier falls, shifting away into nothingness and letting the light of the moon and stars finally shine through.

CHAPTER
TWENTY-FIVE

There's no time for sleep once we get back to campus, though. Riding back took hours, with Blaire waving me away and saying she'd find her own way back, whatever that meant. There wasn't room for her on the bike but I would have made it work.

My arms were limp trying to hold on to Theo, and I halfway debated spending the night at the motel, in the same room.

"I can make it back," he assures me. "I took a cat nap at the motel and slept in a fine tent in the Highlands. Bed of furs, Yas. Bed of furs." He bent to kiss me then shoved his helmet over his head. "I thought about taking you there."

"To the Highlands?"

"No," he says. "On those furs."

I'm blushing before we jet off toward Andora.

Exams are right around the corner, and classes start

tomorrow morning as soon as the sun rises. If we get a few hours of sleep tonight then we're gonna be lucky.

And how in the world is Theo going to explain his highlander style hair to everyone when we get back?

With Gus safely tucked into my shirt, the engine is a lull and I might have dozed off a few times during the drive home. The landscape shifts into those rolling hills, visible even in the night, and the knot in my chest slowly loosens.

Another thirty minutes and we park in the campus lot, back in his usual parking space.

Theo cuts the engine. "We're doing it now?" he clarifies.

The jar. The statue. The trapped god. "We shouldn't waste time. The sooner we get him trapped in his final resting place, the better I'll feel," I reply.

"Then we better get on it."

He helps me off the bike, my legs wobbling to the point where I lose my balance and knock into him.

"You're like a baby deer," Theo murmurs. He pushes the hair out of my face. "So delicate."

"I can't believe you came for me." I shake my head. "You know I tried to leave you in the motel so you'd be safe, right? I didn't want you to get hurt."

"*You* know I told you I would fight for you. Better get used to it. I'm not going anywhere." With our helmets tucked away, Theo links our hands.

Together, we take the Horned God to the center of campus. Ensuring the jar is closed and sealed with a sigil of protection, Theo works the magic to entomb the jar inside the statue. The metal melts away to reveal an empty space inside the body of the Cleric and we set the jar down, entombing him in his own likeness.

"It's sad. It's fitting," I call out loud.

"You did what you had to do," Theo answers. "Try not to feel bad."

I chuckle softly. "Of course I feel bad. Even if we can't see him in the jar, he's in there. Somewhere. Stuck. How do you always know what I'm feeling?"

"I'm not an empath but your face gives you away. Not to mention your kind heart. He got what came to him, Yas."

When I turn to look at Theo, his arms are crossed over his chest, still every bit the powerful warrior.

Yes, karma is certainly at play. Now it's time for me to live my life the way I want. Whatever comes.

Strong arms wrap around me from behind and by the time I turn around to face the very handsome young man said muscular arms belong to, Theo has me off my feet and spinning in a circle.

"I did it," he exclaims, nipping at my hair as he spins me.

I'm laughing, breathless, by the time he sets me on my feet. His lips claim mine a second later and take the last brain cells left in my head, too. Leaving me nothing but the desire to hold him close and finish what he's starting.

"What did you do?" I murmur when he finally pulls back.

"I passed my exams." Theo winks at me. "Thanks to a certain someone who is an amazing teacher. The studying paid off, Yas. I don't know how you did it, but you managed to get through my thick skull and the information stuck this time!"

I stare at him. "You passed? You're not going to fail?"

He winks at me. "Honey, I'm here to stay. I spoke to all my professors and they're so impressed with my grades for midterms that they're willing to work with me on everything else."

"That's amazing!" I kiss him again and rise on my tiptoes to press my lips more fully against his. "I think you just needed the right incentive to do the work yourself," I argue out of principle. "What do you want to do to celebrate?"

I have more than a few things in mind but none of them are acceptable to discuss in polite company.

Joy fills me when Theo smiles and reaches forward to press his lips to my forehead. Off in the distance are a couple of Helena's friends who still don't seem to believe Theo is with another girl. They eye me, not even trying to be discreet.

They don't bother me anymore.

Let people talk if they want to talk. They haven't walked in my shoes, not even close, so if the best they can do is gossip about what an odd couple we make, then it's no skin off me.

I've got Theo, and after a week of studying and hanging out, getting to know each other even better and, yeah...*that*...we're settling into a rhythm.

Andora Academy is my place. X House is my place.

"Let's head to The Shed. This is definitely cause for a celebration." He releases his hold on me and tugs me in the direction of the parking lot.

"You want to head to The Shed?" I ask. "I am always down for milkshakes, but it seems like there are better places for a special celebration."

"Maybe. Unless you don't think passing my exams is anything special." He looks so adorably pouty I laugh.

Rather than play into his joke, I knock my knuckles against his chest. "You better stop your teasing, bad boy."

I really don't want to make a huge deal about Theo passing his exams because, let's face it, he's smart. He could have done it on his own without any help from me if he'd focused and found a way to study that makes sense for his learning style.

He's got the talent and the intelligence to make it far in this world and do literally whatever he wants. If he wants to be a high priest or something even greater, he can do it.

"Let's just say that we're going to start at The Shed and see where things go from there," he offers, with a look promising so much more. "Okay with you?"

Our hands are linked and I snuggle closer as we fall into step beside one another. "It works for me," I reply. *More* than ready to see where things go.

Although the connection between us started off as a ruse, a mutually beneficial agreement, this is real. The feelings are real between us. The same ones I felt so sure were only on my side are returned and it's nothing short of magic.

The Shed is filled with students who have the same idea we do. They're out celebrating the end of midterms.

We grab a booth toward the back of the room and order two strawberry milkshakes.

It's fitting, it's retro, and it's perfect for us. This time I'm not leaving room for any of his friends to join us, either. At least, no one like Becky or Piper. Or Courtney or Kim.

"How did your test go this morning?" I ask once we're settled. "Seems like you got the grade for that one early."

Theo shrugs, looking pleased with himself. "I charmed the professor into letting me see mine early. It seems the confidence of knowing almost every answer on my alchemy exam gave me a certain charisma she was powerless against."

"Oh okay, Mr. Big Ego." I lean forward to brush my nose against his. "But you're right. There's no way she could say no to you. Every answer?"

"Yup, every answer. You should have seen the way I turned lead into gold today. Everyone was impressed."

"You know," I tell him on our way out the door once we're done, "I'll still help you study for your next big test."

"You think I need it?" he teases.

"I think you've got this and a little extra reading with a good study partner doesn't hurt anyone." Our shoulders bump together as we walk. "I can think of a good one for you, someone who doesn't mind extra reading."

Theo leads us away from the parking lot and I have to wonder what's going on. I could have sworn we were heading out for an early evening drive, maybe even a stroll through the gardens near the villa.

Theo has been surprisingly closed lipped about our plans tonight and I have to wonder what kind of surprises he has up his sleeve.

"Oh, you know someone?" he asks.

"I might. And *you're* being sneaky tonight," I whisper.

"Me?" He points innocently to his chest with his free hand. "I'm just happy. Am I allowed to be happy, Yas?"

"More than you realize." Both of us are.

This is a new page turned for us at Andora Academy and one I never would have expected. I've got the guy. I've got the grades. I've got friends, and they see me for me. They see me for what I have to offer and not just my magic.

Between Theo and Blaire, our table at lunch is always filled and people are more than willing to get to know me and give me a chance.

I'm learning and growing.

We make it back to my dorm and I stifle the groan of surprise that he's dropping me off for the night. Until I turn to him and notice the sparkle of mischief back in his gaze.

"What is it?" I ask cautiously.

He breaks eye contact only to reach into his bag and pulls out a highlander romance novel, the next in the same series I'd started with sexy Seamus and his tribe of hot Scots. I suck in a breath.

I haven't read that one yet. I'd been waiting until

after exams finished before I bought the paperback and treated myself to a retreat between the pages.

"I want you to know that I started reading the series, and I have tons to talk to you about. I need to catch you up about my time in the first book." Theo taps the cover. "I experienced some *very* interesting things in there. Some things I figure you'll want to know about."

His voice has dropped low and it skitters through my veins like liquid lightning. My knees quake together.

"You read the book without me?"

"I did because I know it will give us plenty to discuss. Plenty to experience together." He nibbles on my earlobe before sucking it between his lips in a way designed to break past my guard.

"For some reason I know you don't want to discuss anything. You really are a bad boy," I whisper.

"I'm just getting started. I figure it's time for you to see how bad I can be. And for me to see you splayed naked on a bed of furs. Not a moment to waste." He sets me with a mock stern look.

This time I make the first move and kiss him. It's a promise. Of intimacy and sex, of closeness, and of whatever else our future holds.

A promise I am more than willing to embrace.

The End

NEVER PREY

Little Red Riding Hood had a big, bad wolf... I have four.

I didn't even know werewolves existed. Or that the story my parents used to tell me about a mythical Moon Goddess was real.

But it's true—all of it—and that means the part about her gifting me with only twenty-five years of life is too. With my final birthday looming, I'm on a mission to save myself, but that mission ends up throwing me in the middle of two warring werewolf packs.
Now, the rival alphas and their two betas have me in their sights.

Torin, Noble, Mathis, and Dax are sexier than sin, but they're hunters, killers, some of the most powerful men in the shifter and human world…

And they want a taste of me.

They're in for a surprise: I might not be a wolf like them, but I'm never prey.

Bestselling authors Harper A. Brooks and Brea Viragh have created a world of magic, heat, and bloodthirsty wolves. In this paranormal romance series, the heroine will end up with more than one love interest.

MORE BOOKS BY HARPER A. BROOKS

REAPER REBORN

Death Wish

Death Trap

Death Match

Death Deals

Death Sentence

Till Death

Christmas Spirits: A Holiday Novella

Halfling for Hire: A Short Story Collection

BAD WOLVES

Never Prey

Never Submit

Never Tamed

Bad Wolves: The Complete Collection

KINGDOM OF MONSTERS

Shadow Prince: A Prequel

Cruel Shadows

Necessary Evil

Wicked Reign

Vile Creatures (Kingdom of Monsters Complete Collection)

SIN DEMONS

Playing with Hellfire

Hell in a Handbasket

All Shot to Hell

To Hell and Back

When Hell Freezes Over

Hell on Earth

Snowball's Chance in Hell: A Holiday Novella

Hell or Highwater: A Holiday Novella

Darkest Sin: Part One (Sin Demons Complete Collection)

Darkest Sin: Part Two (Sin Demons Complete Collection)

MOON KISSED

Wolf Hunter

Wolf Tamer

Wolf Protector

Moon Kissed: The Complete Collection

LOVE & LORE

Primal Hunger

Primal Prey

KINGS OF EDEN

Kings of Eden

Stolen Paradise

Ruthless Lies

SHIFTERS UNLEASHED

Tiger Claimed

Wolf Marked

STAND ALONES

His Haven

Eternally Yours

Monstrous: A Monster Romance Novella

Monstrous Bond: A Monster Romance Novella

Immortal Throne

Spelling Disaster

About the Author

Harper A. Brooks may be a Jersey girl at heart, but now she likes to hideout in the mountains of Virginia with bigfoot and all his little woodland friends. Even though classic authors have always filled her bookshelves, she finds her writing muse drawn to the dark, magical, and romantic. When she isn't creating entire worlds with sexy shifters or legendary love stories, you can find her either with a good cup of coffee in hand or at home snuggling with her furry, four-legged son, Sammy.

RONE AWARD WINNER
USA TODAY BESTSELLING AUTHOR
INTERNATIONAL BESTSELLING AUTHOR

Join Harper's reader group for exclusive content, sneak-peeks, giveaways, and more!

facebook.com/HarperABrooks
twitter.com/HarperABrooks
instagram.com/harperabrooks

Made in the USA
Middletown, DE
03 May 2024